FRACTURE

SASHA FAULKS

For Peter

'There are more things in heaven and earth, Horatio

Than are dreamt of in your philosophy…'

Hamlet Act 1 Scene 5

What we have is time and space, and no other instructions.

LIST OF CHARACTERS

Arthur Smith	Shopkeeper
Noley Naismith	Arthur's partner
Steve (-)	Arthur's friend
Amber Archer	Curator (Arthur's wife)
Angelica Archer	Curator (Arthur's daughter)
Torran Smith	Curator (Arthur's grandson)
Rini Sanchez	Curator (Arthur's friend)
Reggie Sanchez	Governor (Rini's brother)
Clem Curran	Governor (Rini's friend)
Dillan Archer	Governor (Amber's brother)
Tam (-)	Governor (Rini's colleague)
Dee D'Abruzzo	Governor (Rini's colleague)
Demmy D'Abruzzo	Governor (Dee's twin sister)
Ben (-)	Governor (Demmy's husband)
Joe Solomon	Curator (Rini's friend)
Jade (-)	Curator (Torran's girlfriend)
Mindy	First spaniel
Mindy 2	Second spaniel
Mabel	Third spaniel
Bryony	Fourth spaniel

CONTENTS

ARTHUR (I)

Rini could fly away, but she chooses to come back with the unfathomable trust of the goshawk that, against nature's odds, beats its wings through the air and returns to my grateful glove.

We're a generation apart—what you might call a world apart—and we met in her world when she showed more human grace than I had ever experienced, then or since, by offering a foster home to my grandson and, when the powers that be decided she wasn't a suitable mother, she never lost sight of him or his foolish grandfather in the years that followed.

You might say she undertook a much wider role in foster care than any authority could have granted.

In over-ripe old age, I'm glad I didn't meet Rini when I was young when I would have tried to charm her into bed. Now I am just stupidly grateful that she is my best friend. I use the word 'charm' loosely as I'm unsure what the alternative might be. Like a lot of lonely, idiotic old men, I have lost count of my conquests. I used to compare myself favourably with my male counterparts in the natural world, doing evolution a favour by spreading my seed. Now, I understand I've been the worst of prowling tomcats, forever on a mission to fill my belly and empty my balls. In my defence, there were one or two alley she-cats who turned their tails in my face and made my mission an irresistible challenge. Resistance, of course, would have been the more honourable challenge, but we often only learn the value of honour with age.

The woman who became my wife was no alley cat, showing a type of tenacity that chimed with my way of looking at life at that time. I met her shortly after I had discovered there was a parallel universe right next to mine, accessible through a nondescript clearing in the woods: a tear in the membrane that separated our worlds, one of maybe countless fractures in our universe. My passage to liberation. There must be something in the make-up of a mad, sad individual like myself that made me ripe for the discovery because I have never met another person from my world who has journeyed between this one and another, unless they simply keep their secret as guarded as I do. This is hard to believe, as most of the fools I have come across are all too ready to share their confidences: to break open their life experiences like monkeys breaking open melons to impress us with the contents. Show-offs and charlatans in the main, to a man (or woman).

Amber found me pissing against a tree—a dying oak that had been struck by lightning, so my bladder-watering was affording it no real disrespect. This was a time when 'dropping out' was more unusual and less groovy than it was set to become, on either side of our tracks. She asked me what I was doing. She had a quizzical, humorous face under a mop of wild black hair, and a gap between her front teeth that was almost as big as a tooth itself, which added to her allure for someone like me who approved of the beauty of imperfection. She knew well enough what I was doing, which was why I didn't mind turning around and exposing my piss-part to her. It was, after all, not the era of political correctness. She laughed like she needed the merriment cure. She soon got the whole answer: I was wasting my time in her woods, looking for berries, mushrooms, and kindling; and finding any excuse not to be at home where I was expected to help out at my father's ironmonger's. She learned that I built shelters between the legs of trees, and often slept in them, or under the leaf-shielded stars. I wasn't inclined to encourage her, as I was busy working on the wavering morals of a buxom barmaid that summer (several years my senior), but she made it her business to search me out, and, by and by, her daft questions became her part in proper conversations. Eventually, we had little need of talk at all as she tacitly joined me foraging, wading through streams, smoking cigarettes. To my shame, perhaps, I don't remember the first time I had her, but I do recall the season of easy copulation that followed. I have always believed Amber might have made someone the most wonderful wife, but it should never have been me.

It was inevitable that her fecundity would have its day in our once primordial forest setting where seeds had been popping and larvae had been hatching around us with splendid, irrepressible regularity since time immemorial. Our sweet and peaceful friendship was shattered, however, like a frozen puddle smashed with a broken tree branch: the branch appearing metaphorically in the fist of her older brother Dillan. He wasn't an overtly threatening chap, but he arrived at her side one day, knowing Amber was pregnant before I did, which meant I would never have the chance to find out if I might have liked him, or to properly trust his sister ever again.

4

A baby on the way (or 'a bun in the oven,' as my parents used to say) changed my course of history forever.

I might be forgiven for craving the indulgence of sympathy at this point, as I don't think Amber's course was altered much by the arrival of our baby Angelica: the roundest, most wrinkly baby I had ever seen; two weeks late into the world, and as much like an over-cooked—or over-steamed—bun as you might imagine. It was a blessing for her overwrought young mother, however, that she took her time to truly wake up to her life *ex utero,* and granted her a full six weeks of almost unbroken sleep until (I'm guessing) she had used up her foetal reserves, and found the need to unleash her hefty vocal demands for nourishment upon the world. Amber and Angelica inhabited a world where motherhood was almost inevitably the pinnacle of their lives' ambition: both born into the generally guaranteed status of curatorship rather than governance, neither possessing the family investment nor the inherent curiosity and intelligence required to change their lot. Like Rini, only somehow (and to my eternal shame) occupying a very different plot in my heart space than she would come to inhabit.

My course of history was altered like an oak crashing down into a stream that otherwise would have made its way to the sea. A stream whose natural progress was brought to a gurgling halt, to be redefined as a shallow body of water liable to run dry, or even to stagnate. There might have been barriers in the society where I came from to prevent the son of an ironmonger looking 'up,' and changing his lot; but, in my case, I had been granted a place at Cambridge university to study English literature. It could just as easily have been Natural Sciences—or whatever else I'd set my cap at, as a teacher had told my timorously proud parents. I think they liked the idea of their son studying a subject unequivocally about book-learning, rather than just 'the outdoors' that had taken up so much of his time as a child who made himself more of a nuisance by his absence than by his presence; so I opted for the former rather than the latter. As Fate would have it, the choice became moot, as impending fatherhood loomed like a landscape of hospitals and council houses right outside my front door, rather than one of colleges and libraries in some faraway city: a city that became less and less of a reality for me as the weeks and months of Amber's pregnancy rolled by.

My parents didn't know. They couldn't know. I married Amber in a formal registry building at the insistence of her brother Dillan one Saturday afternoon when I'd managed to be let off working in the shop; and he oversaw our removal from occasional, casual accommodation in the woods into the formality of social housing: an estate where rent was cheap because the inhabitants lived in a type of commune. She wore a voluminous striped outfit that was more of a tent than a dress, but less of a tent than the one made from branches and moss wherein we had conceived our child. Her sister-in-law threw homemade confetti that stuck to our skin and even made its way into my underwear. My mum asked what it was that had caused a stain in the laundry. I told her I'd left a pen in my jeans pocket, and she believed me.

On the day Angelica was born, I missed a history exam. I look back and wonder why I didn't just go AWOL straight away, rather than hanging around as much as I did in order not to miss the birth. At the time, I was still fond enough of Amber, and was touched by her clever transformation from just another grinning girl into a young woman swelling sweetly by degrees, and about to join what I considered nature's most exalted rank of motherhood. Her labour was long, and I had the foresight to go into school to tell my teacher that my father had taken ill, and I wasn't going to be able to sit any more exams that summer. I asked them, please, to respect the family's privacy and not to intrude, as my imminent failure to complete my A-Levels, and therefore not to go to university, was a source of regret at home. The truth of the matter was that my parents barely noticed if I was 'out' at school, in the pub, or in the woods (on either side of my double life). I was coming and going as I pleased, and, all the while, Amber accepted that there would be days and nights when I wouldn't be living under the same roof as her in her brother-borne house. She knew her baby's father was going to be, at best, an unreliable catch, and, at worst, a deserter, so she had of me what I deigned to spare her; and when our daughter was eventually hauled out of the oven of her womb, Amber yielded almost instantly to the superior care of her neighbours in the commune. Not that we didn't have many hours together rapt in wonder at the little person we had created, who had her mother's dark slick of baby hair that remained stuck across the front of her head even when it had rubbed off the back, giving her a look of Adolf Hitler (mercifully unheard of in Amber's world; and, in any case, no one would have paid much attention to the rants of an unremarkable man of questionable social pedigree). She also had my overly full lips and slightly recessive chin, poor child. Most detrimentally of all, she had teenage parents whose commitment to a life together lasted about as long as the cake one of her aunties had unboxed to eat with sparkling wine on our wedding day.

Rini once asked me how I managed to live this double life. (She got to know me well enough, I think, not to question the *why*, but the practicality of the *how* continued to perplex her). I don't know which came first: my inability to commit to the people on either side of my parallel lives, or their lack of commitment to me, which made my frequent absence not unusual. Did my parents ever really *care* about my thwarted ambition to go to a top university? They accepted the news that I hadn't passed any of my exams like they accepted any minor announcement I might make, such as the regular possibility of my not coming home that night. I knew other boys at school for whom either of the above scenarios would have caused ructions of climactic proportions, but not so in my household. Most of the time, I was glad of my liberty—especially when I wanted to be out and about in the service of my libido—but there were times when their apathy gave me pause for thought. I wondered if my parents had been caught out by the arrival of a baby Arthur much like I was by a baby Angelica, and they had felt obligated to live their lives in a more straitened fashion than they would have wanted: my father committing to the family business that had been his father's before him, invalided without glory out of active wartime service with two broken legs when a fellow private had inadvertently run him over; supported by my mother in her housecoat, emerging when summoned from her kitchen of unappetising smells where she harboured pencil drawings of mannequins in glamorous dresses on the back of her grocery packets. Looking back, I imagine one of them wished he'd been able to fly planes while the other wished she were living a life turned out in the fashions of Christian Dior, so perhaps their status quo was a precursor to my own suffocated ambition. We possessed lots of photographs of the three of us enjoying my babyhood, staged in a variety of sunny locations, none of which I could remember with any degree of accuracy without the aid of a celluloid prompt. I think as I succumbed to the gravitational pull from boy- to manhood, my parents gave in to the weakness of their attachment to me in an equal and opposite way: culminating in an unspiteful, but suboptimal, disregard for me, and me for them.

So, as I explained to Rini, *that* was how I 'managed' not to implicate my parents in my life with Amber, or indeed with any other friend of either sex to any significant degree. They asked me few questions, and I told them almost as many lies. They both died (my father of a heart attack, and my mother, subsequently, in the *Canary Heights* home for the elderly where she resided in her final years, listening to the wireless all day without any discernible desire to converse with her fellow interns), ignorant of the wife and child I'd had before I'd met Denise, Rita, or Andrea—or the especially luckless Noley who copped for the unenviable baton of partnership with me in running the shop, as she happened to be the lass I was laying at the time I took it over. I'm not convinced my parents would have turned much of a grey hair at the news that, somewhere in a great beyond—even more remote than their Spitfire skies and Parisian catwalks—I had briefly lived another life that had created them a granddaughter.

As for Amber, she was little more than a child herself when she became a wife and mother. (I will be a man-child until my dying breath: no amount of progeny would have altered that, or rebranded me as a responsible role model). She appeared to enjoy attending to her baby daughter as much as she did organising the crockery in her cupboards, or listening to her vinyl records. In my world, the 1960s were unleashing a new wave of music that wasn't yet in evidence in the cafés that Amber and her friends frequented, or in the commune where they lived. The pace of life there seemed to continue much as it had when I had first been introduced to it, with musical recordings of a largely classical or folky nature, played by both the young and the old alike. I might spend an afternoon weeding the allotment, with Amber in serene attendance, Angelica on her hip, and then return to an all-night party on a street near my parents' shop, dropping acid in the hope I might experience some sort of freedom in my own head, as I was now unlikely to find it any other way. A new world? I had been trapped like a fly who had found its way out from under a jam jar only to land in a spider's web!

So, two worlds weren't enough for you? Rini once said, when I was describing my drug-taking escapades. I think perhaps she was right.

The best pill at that stage of my life, however, was the contraceptive pill, as it cloaked coercion in the respectable mantle of choice; not perhaps how this ground-breaking liberator of women's social circumstances should be remembered, but, if I'm brutally honest, it just meant I didn't have to beg for sex as much as I had before. It came too late for Amber who may not have chosen it anyway, as there appeared to be a different sort of morality around raising babies in her world, as well as in terms of holding the family unit together. Or so it seemed to me at the time. If I had been inclined to look more closely at 'normal' families at home, however, I might have found our worlds to be not so different. I was growing tired of Amber's increasingly reluctant acquiescence in the bedroom we shared with an often-wakeful Angelica, and began to think of all the girls closer to home that I could be bedding. Once I had set my mind on this alternative course of action I was unstoppable, and somewhat insatiable. That's not to say I didn't experience hot pangs of guilt as I made my untimely exits from the little house in the commune, closed down in the decency of slumber, but these were readily extinguished by my sense of the ice-cold absurdity that I had been married off to a sweet but rather dim-witted girl before I had even turned twenty.

Soon my already perforated conscience was ruptured into ragged holes, and I was deceiving more than just my hapless parents with my duplicitous existence. Once I had successfully got together with a girl called Denise, who was soon to be supplanted by Rita, I was less and less inclined to wander back to the commune through the breach in the woods to visit my wife and baby daughter. These weren't young women who wanted to be messing about in trees, making tents, and rescuing birds that had fallen out of nests: they were from a cohort of students and budding professionals who prompted in me the notion that there was more to life than selling rawl plugs and rat poison whilst intermittently sloping off to my strange other world of sleepy domesticity. It was Andrea who had the most impact. I would say she was the woman who broke my heart, but it was much less conventionally romantic than that. She was studying law at Durham university (having 'failed' to get into Oxford) and, between naked capers and smoking joints on the carpet of the attic bedroom of her parents' house, she used to tease me about my lack of ambition, even for my academic inferiority. I told her I'd had a place at Cambridge two years earlier, but she didn't believe me. I didn't know how to convince her this was the truth, so I used to pit my wits against hers by sparking heated intellectual debates at every opportunity after rigorous research and banging her breathless. After one particular session on booze and drugs, I dreamt (or imagined) that I had strangled her with a pair of her own tights to shut her up, because she had been taunting me for being a numbskull; and I reckon this must have shocked me into a different reality. I needed to prove something to myself, not to Andrea, who was still alluring and willing, but a constant reminder of my failings rather than my potential. I enrolled into college to retake my A-Levels, and spent the summer before my first term started in reasonably regular and meek attendance at the little house inhabited by Amber, and Angelica who was now toddling and calling me Dadda. I had briefly lost the lead in my pencil, the means of shooting my arrow; and Amber unwittingly granted me the forbearance to regain this vindication of my manhood over a warm season of unchallenged potency, both intellectually and physically. I knew I didn't love her, or Andrea, but I realised I would never be content with a simple, wildflower girl like Amber while there was a world of *exotica flora* out there, like clever Andrea, waiting to be plucked and pressed between the pages of my life story.

Amber was sweetly excited about my new sense of purpose. She had never really understood the gravity of my turning my back on a university career: it seemed to have very little to do with her role as a mother and a member of the commune; and she assumed I was the son of a shopkeeper somewhere in a nearby town who might aspire to run a similar business closer to home one day. There were one or two reasonably well-educated members of the commune, but they hadn't amounted to much, or been able to prove themselves beyond their allotted status of curatorship rather than governance in their society. There was a librarian who had a university degree, but it was clear he had scaled the expected peak of his ambition by running the library. Equally, a teacher who was destined only to use her degree in 'the old languages' (which seemed to include

Latin and Greek) to instruct children in the commune at primary level. Few seemed to seriously question their lot. There were doctors and professors who were Governors, and who clearly commanded a greater degree of respect, but certainly no one to whom I felt I might disclose that there was at least one other world out there. Looking back, I admit my reservations in that respect were probably rooted in selfishness, as *escape* from the domestic drudgery of the ordered little estate where Amber seemed so at home digging vegetables and washing other people's clothes was always on the periphery of my intentions, even on long summer days when I'd been busy mending fences, painting walls, and cutting back trees with some of the other husbands and fathers. It was the general opinion that I was bright (for someone with limited career prospects), but there was a sense that my increasing periods of absence were causing consternation amongst the more influential visitors to the commune. Amber's parents were dead, so her brother Dillan assumed a role of seniority within the family, not least because he had been able to join the ruling class of governorship by qualifying as a paediatrician. He lived with his wife and children in a large house in a more affluent neighbourhood, but he was a frequent visitor who kept a brotherly eye on his sister, and afforded her his professional peace of mind by checking on Angelica's progress whenever he came by. I imagine he was as well-intentioned as he had been on the day he rounded us up in the woods, but I noticed Amber was always a little unsettled after he'd called, as though his assessment of our daughter's development was less than reassuring. I was no help, as Angelica seemed like any other child of her age that I had come across, which was admittedly an insignificant handful, whom I assumed wouldn't necessarily learn to talk or co-ordinate themselves particularly effectively until they were 'older'. It may have been concern about the child's well-being that brought forward the inevitable summons one afternoon to meet Dillan for a man-to-man chat. I had just turned nineteen, and was sat opposite a chap nearly ten years older than me who instilled more fear in me than my own father, despite the offer of a shared bottle of beer. He told me that *Gregory* was planning his retirement from running the library, and it was a good time to start showing his successor the ropes, and that I seemed like the ideal candidate, particularly as it would give me the encouragement I 'maybe needed' to be a permanent presence in Amber's and Angelica's lives. He suggested it was time for my parents to manage without me in their business (Amber must have given him her own cobbled-together idea of my situation), and that with the sponsorship of someone like himself (a Governor) and, with me being the father of a young child in the commune, I had a strong chance of getting the post. I listened, I nodded, I agreed, much as I had done when I had been sat down several years earlier and told that I was going to be put forward for the Oxbridge examinations at school. Dillan knew nothing of my A-Level aspirations at this point, but I sensed it was only a matter of time before there would be more searching questions asked about where I was studying and, more devastatingly, where I came from—and regularly disappeared to— without his sister's knowledge.

For the first time in my life I felt a weight of responsibility on my shoulders. I wandered back home through the woods with Dillan's beer sitting like a cold pool of despair in my belly. I decided I would break the truth to my parents and explain my predicament. What should I do? Should I stay or should I go? Who else could I ask for advice?

When I got home, there was a girl called Alison waiting for me in my mum's kitchen, making herself a cup of tea, turning inquisitive brown eyes my way, and asking if we might do the assignment on *Hamlet* together. It was a Wednesday afternoon, and the shop was shut. I could make out the muffled suggestion of a game of cricket on my father's radio through the walls several rooms away, and my mother was nowhere to be seen. I sat at the table, and talked all sorts of nonsense that had nothing to do with Shakespeare with Alison, who twirled a strand of honey-blonde hair between her fingers while I drifted, and tried to imagine a way forward where I might either escape the ties of one of my worlds or possibly unite the bonds of both. My focus came back to brown eyes, and the kick I got from flirting with an intellectual female, and declared we should abandon tea and go for a walk in the woods. Alison was too decent—and too preoccupied with our academic endeavour—to let me undo her bra on this particular occasion, but I was prepared to bide my time.

When my mind was made up, I felt the same buzz I'd experienced whenever I'd narrowly missed being clipped by a car on running across the road, or when I'd dodged out of the path of a falling tree (which had

12

happened to me more than the average bloke). I had outsmarted Fate. I studied hard, and got a place at Durham university to read English and to catch up with Andrea (and to bed and best her, academically) before she graduated and left, and we went our separate ways.

My first-class degree, as it turned out, was the culmination of my career, as I returned home to languish in a permanent state of awaiting the right opportunity—believing it might manifest itself any moment without any further investment from me or my parents—which never amounted to more than accepting that my lot was to take over the running of my father's business. However, there always seemed to be somebody (and thankfully she was usually female) who found something of interest in a man reading classical literature behind the counter of a corner shop. I don't think I'm a boaster (selfish, perhaps, but not conceited), but I often found myself contemplating just how interesting I was, compared to the next Joe, given I was a first-class academic who had also set foot in a parallel universe. Either (or both) of these accolades was the stuff of other people's fantasies.

As years went by, I became as psychologically estranged from Amber and her commune as I was from my halls of residence in Durham, and my habitual status quo was to be opening and closing the ironmonger's that still had my father's name over the door (even though he had been dead for twenty years), and making my escape into the woods. I came back full circle to the solace of my childhood, which was to be outdoors and at the mercy of Mother Nature, inviting her to lead me in whatever direction she saw fit, the incorrigible champion of hers that I cast myself as. More than the company of other people, I wanted the company of wild, untamed creatures: primarily birds (especially hawks), which eventually took its toll on what you might describe as my final 'normal' relationship with a woman.

Noley Naismith had been a long-suffering partner, who had done her best to make sense of things when my parents were still alive, and worked hard to draw upon any residual sympathy I might harbour for them. She took pains to remember birthdays and to cook family suppers, as though such attention to detail might serve to light a candle of familial remembrance. It didn't. I tried to explain that it was impossible to rekindle a past that had never existed, but she found this notion too sad to contemplate, and maybe didn't always believe was true. She was one of the kindest, most gracious people I had ever met (until Rini, of course, but she was a whole different animal), and used to worry about the house being too draughty for my elderly mother, or about our bed squeaking too much when we were having sex. I watched her putting a stack of shock-absorbing beer mats under the legs of our bed, and informed her that the old woman was practically deaf and slept like a corpse, so we shouldn't concern ourselves too much. I hadn't the heart to add that my parents had been turning deaf ears to more of my sexual antics over the years than the brewery had printed mats, or the barmaid had pulled pints to put on them. Hyperbolic, perhaps, but not so far removed from the truth.

Noley never had to suffer the indignity of my infidelity with another woman, but finally reached the end of her tether when I announced that my second goshawk, whom I'd named Serena, was about to be moved in for her schooling. I tried to convince her that it was a temporary arrangement, but she had, of course, tolerated this once before, so mine was a poorly constructed defence, and undoubtedly just one of the many annoyances of living under the same roof as me that culminated in her decision to leave. She was 'one for allergies', and was convinced birds in the house affected her weak chest. Dutiful to the last, she waited until my mother had passed away in her care home before she fully relinquished the responsibility she felt towards what might loosely be termed as my family. She moved out, and went to live with her sister on the coast (I don't recall which one) to take on another caretaking role, but this time, I can only imagine, for a worthier recipient.

I accepted this latest change in my fortunes as one of those things that happens in life, or, that loathsome expression of today, 'It is what it is'. It was what it was! I watched spring stretch out its young limbs in readiness for the long walk of summer. A new season would be my mentor; and I could look forward to my immersion in the outdoors, to solitude, and to training my hawk.

A busybody customer took it upon herself to pitch up in the pretence of buying a hammer for her husband, so she could tell me I should be ashamed of myself for not having the decency to put a ring on 'that poor girl's' finger, after all she had done for me and my parents. It seemed that

Noley may have expected more of me than I had ever realised, or perhaps cared to notice. It wasn't as if we were a baby-making kind of a couple. We'd had an early conversation about contraception years before that suggested Noley had an issue with the lining of her womb, meaning she was unlikely to conceive; but I did pause for thought as I put the unlucky husband's hammer back on its sale hook, and concluded that Noley had drawn a pretty short straw when she had ended up with me and mine. There were no more tights in the bathroom, hanging like used prophylactics in the way of the mirror; and no more curly blonde hairs clogging up my manly comb. The latter, it has to be said, did make me sad.

I had met a man in the pub who knew about hawks. His name was Steve, and he generally kept himself to himself, but the advantage of knowing the barmaid well did me a service, as she was adept at linking people in conversation who otherwise wouldn't have made a sociable connection with each other.

Noley called me anti-social until she met Steve, who used the fewest number of words of anyone we had ever come across. There was a quiet generosity about him that impressed me, and I lamented the lack of male friends in my youth when I had been far too distracted by women to seek pleasure in the company of my own sex. However, quiet Steve was here now, fifteen years or so my junior, but nevertheless not repulsed by my company on our long drives in his rusted old Land Rover, with its rubber window seals frilled with lichen, to the hide where we waited for birds. The feathered kind. The notion of raising a hawk to fly back to my glove seemed at first anathema to me: why would anyone want to tame such a free spirit—and such a mighty, majestic free spirt at that? I pictured the circus elephant I had seen on TV that was forced onto its knees by a man with a top hat and whip. Steve struggled with the analogy (he wasn't one for citing from his own imagination, so it was probably a stretch to entertain extracts from mine), but convinced me that I might (just might) be sparing a young hawk from an early death in the wild, and that the bird would one day be released from captivity back into its natural habitat. I wasn't entirely convinced—and I'm guessing neither was Steve, as he ended up working at a hawk conservancy—but, like any person persuaded of the need to make some sort of sport out of the natural world, like any small boy who dissects a frog in order to understand anatomy, I captured and raised both Miranda and Serena under Steve's careful tutelage, and the experience made me (I tentatively believe) a better person. I daren't speculate whether the girls went on to survive or perish without my patronage. I can only hope that it was the former, but, if they did meet untimely deaths on my account, I imagine they might have forgiven me, in the universality of things, for laying on a running buffet of pre-prepared rabbits and mice in my living room to spare them the hardship of hunting—whilst sacrificing my own domestic bliss with an exasperated woman.

Quiet Steve aside, I had no friends to speak of. Running a shop for most of my adult life meant I saw enough people on a daily basis not to consider myself lonely. Eventually, technology brought the concept of online shopping, which seemed to me an entirely preferable way to serve or be served, although I suspect many shopkeepers of my generation wouldn't agree. One day in the woods, years before this came to pass, I confessed to Steve that I wished I had more male friends, and that I'd spent more time pursuing birds of the feathered variety. It was the type of throwaway comment he might have grunted at if we had been drinking pints in the *Oak,* but it seemed to knock him off his guard that day, and he looked uncharacteristically coy. He said, 'You aren't *into* me, man, are you?' which almost made me drop my fishing net for laughing at him. I recovered my composure enough to say, 'Do I strike you as the sort of guy who would be *into* men, Steve?!' to which he replied, 'Well it would fucking creep me out, 'cos you're way too old for me.' We cast our lines for the rest of the afternoon, and went home via a pint or two. I slept on it, and began to work on the conversation I wanted to have with Steve next time I saw him. By the time I did, I'd decided it was a conversation we didn't really need to have. It was still a time when there were people scared of homosexuality, and its link to HIV and AIDS; but not people like me, who generally felt they had dodged a gun-load of bullets after an early life of wanton promiscuity, and just been lucky (or not *un*lucky, depending on which way you looked at life). Steve was gay. Not the loud and proud, banner-waving sort of gay that would 'strut and fret its hour upon the stage,' but a careful-who-you-talk-to-until-you know-where-you-stand sort. I was broadly impressed that I had been allowed into his confidence, despite the clumsiness of my admittance. Once I knew, aspects of his behaviour began to make a different kind of sense. He wasn't just plain anti-social (like me), he just tended to do most of his socialising with members of his own team, and was inclined to keep his own counsel when we were down the local pub. As far as I am able to judge these things, we were good mates. I had never had a close male chum while at school or college (and I wasn't famously *close* with any of my women, for that matter). Steve and I just rubbed along, knowing when to chat and knowing when we needed to let the birds, the river, or the rain do the talking.

One Christmas, he must have been buoyed up by festive spirit (or under the influence of someone else's), as he asked me what my plans were for Christmas dinner. In the normal course of events, my answer would have been eating corned beef sandwiches in the woods, slathered in mustard, washed down with a four-pack of beer and flask of coffee, simply because it was a period when the shop would be closed, and I would have a day or two to myself. Therefore the most acceptable answer I could muster was 'no plans'. Steve said he was cooking lunch for a couple of friends, and I was welcome to join them. I wasn't in the habit of receiving invitations since Noley had left, and taken any social favours I might have been afforded with her, so I was out of practice in how best to turn them down without offending anyone—she was always better at that than me, or, better still, would have gone without me. So I told Steve something along the lines of, 'Could I get back to him?' and mentioned a 'rain check', and, to my relief, he seemed satisfied enough with that.

Despite my disinclination to be persuaded of the joys of the season, it had always been a custom of mine to read *A Christmas Carol* at that time of year. Maybe it was born out of hope retained from my childhood that there would be redemption for all of us, no matter how wrong-minded we'd been; or it could just have been a habit like any other, like a fox returning to an empty chicken coop because it had feasted there once before. That year, it may have been the inspiration for me to gather up my surplus beer and whisky, and a fruit cake that had been brought in by one of my customers, and to turn up on Steve's doorstep. I had no idea of the protocol, but it didn't matter that I had arrived early, as I was given the task of feeding the cat who subsequently decided I was a festive ally, and shadowed me for the rest of the day. Steve had also invited a neighbour who ate her turkey lunch with just a modicum of gratitude which suggested to me that she and Steve were in the habit of looking out for each other, and that today wasn't just an act of seasonal charity. The other guests at his table were David and Seth, who were a couple in the broadest sense of the word, and neither of whom was discomfited by the unkempt, probably screamingly heterosexual older guy that Steve had invited over, so I assumed they knew enough about me and our friendship not to feel the need to ask too many questions. We all shared the usual festive pleasantries, and it was tolerable enough that I managed to make it to the cutting of the fruit cake before I succumbed to the urge to remove the cat from my lap, make my polite excuses, and leave. I said Noley might be calling, none of them knowing that the lone Christmas card on my mantlepiece was from her; and that she wasn't accustomed to making contact (and certainly not telephoning) aside from this annual marker of the one-time connection between us.

I lay in my bed that Christmas night, too full of food and drink to slip effortlessly to sleep, in advance of the Boxing Day walk we'd all said we might meet up for at dinner (but had no firm intention of doing). My insomnia was induced by more than just over-indulgence that day. I was usually a good sleeper—much to Noley's annoyance, as she used to keep her bedside cabinet stocked with potions, eye-masks, and sleeping pills to assist in sending her off—and I always knew there was a fathomable underlying reason if ever I found myself at odds with the divine *Hypnos*. It was as straightforward as taking off a childhood shoe and ejecting the bit of grit that was impeding a walk. I just needed to focus on identifying the impediment—which was rarely a full belly—and removing it. I began a groggy forensic analysis of my long Christmas lunch, and the things that were discussed as we'd shovelled soft meat and hot gravy into our wine-numbed mouths, sharing more with our strange and disparate company than we might normally have done: or certainly in the case of the old lady, David, and Seth, as Steve and I pretty much kept our usual counsel. The drink made us quiet men all the more attentive listeners than talkers, and we learned that May had once been a cabaret dancer (or at least *I* learned this, having never come across her before) which

18

required a bold imagination as she now sported pendulous breasts under a grubby cardigan and a hairy chin. We also learned that David and Seth—who were both about Steve's age—had a desire to be parents, either via surrogacy or adoption, but they weren't confident that this would ever come to pass. Not without a seismic change in people's attitudes, they said. More's the pity, May had added, as she lamented the indecent number of opposite-sex parents who made such a bad job of it. We had toasted a future where David and Seth might look forward to being fathers with no one making a fuss about it, and a good year to come: the latter being standard festive banter.

As I rolled over, and my eyelids finally began to droop, I realised the bit of grit had been dislodged from my sandal, and was tinkling down the drain somewhere in the foggy water-closet of my mind. It was the realisation that it was *I* who had made the bad job of parenting that the old woman had been referring to at the festive dinner table.

I was the one being visited by the ghost of Christmas past—and the judgement wasn't a favourable one.

I wasn't intent on disrupting anyone's Boxing Day agenda the following day, or causing any more distress than I may have already done some twenty-odd years earlier; but I knew I had to rediscover the breach in woods: that gateway to my closest otherworld neighbour—at least one more time—to find my daughter, and to make some kind of peace with her.

RINI (I)

My name is Rini Sanchez, and my story begins where all stories should—with my childhood.

As I write, we are living under the cloud of a pandemic: our streets feel as desolate as an eastern block winter, and our temperaments tested in ways we haven't experienced before. The faces of the strangers who pass me by have become as stark as the daily news bulletins: some look anxious, while many appear curiously serene, as though they have been relieved of their usual oppressive concerns, and may never think the same way about them again.

For me, when my mind is full or my heart is heavy, I can draw upon memories of a happy childhood to give me comfort. I remember my parents shovelling snow from our doorstep while we slept snugly in our beds—or, rather, my brother and sister slept while I rested in a state of blissful half-slumber, enjoying eavesdropping on my parents' breathless and happy conversation, conducted to the rhythm of their spades slicing sharply through impacted snow. Or (something that you may find perverse), the memory of the day that I dispatched my sister Becks' hamster that had a tumour on its back. In this instance, the poor little creature needed to be put out of its misery, not least the misery of Becks' constant poking and prodding which was intended, I think, to ease both the suffering of the tiny thing and that of its grief-stricken owner. I suspect any benefit was afforded to my sister alone, and not her hapless hamster. Reggie, our brother, felt sick at the thought of touching a diseased animal, and had decided we would do better to cast it out into the garden to let his interpretation of nature take its course. I did the deed by gently compressing its tiny chest until it lay lifeless yet victorious in my hand, having won its small but necessary battle against the fickle nature of human children.

We wept in a huddle, united in the aftershock of our trespass into the grim world of adulthood, and the type of trauma it might bring. Reggie was actually physically sick, but subsequently donated an old crayon tin from his bedroom to serve as the hamster's coffin. Becks declared she would never want another pet in her life ever again (until a kitten arrived the following summer as a reward for her good school grades). Reggie quickly forgot the whole episode, and didn't enjoy being reminded of it. This was the nature of our young lives together: my brother, my sister, and me.

Years later, cast as one of life's Curators, I was to become an archivist at the university, while my brother became the leader of the council that found homes for the dispossessed, and my sister became a lecturer. I don't believe either Reggie or Becks cared deeply about, in his case, lessening the despair of the homeless, or, in hers, inspiring hope through education, but caring isn't necessarily the cornerstone of governorship. However, I loved them both more than they would ever know—and certainly more than they loved me in return.

As I grew up, I realised that being useful to others was more important to me than almost anything else in my life.

My best friend at school was a girl called Clem Curran who, compared to me, was clever and quick-witted. I didn't particularly enjoy school, but every morning when I woke up, my closed-down, night-time face was soon alive with elation that I was going to see Clem again that day—to bask in her friendship, and to play some part in her escapades. She had only one arm or, should I say, *hand,* as her right arm finished in a neat, smooth stump below her elbow. Her ability to function so well without the support of all nature's bodily fixtures and fittings was a thing of fascination, almost pride, to me. She could flip and fasten the buckles on her school satchel in half the time it would have taken most other people, and it remains nestled in my memory of her like the feat of a gymnast. Her satchel was then thrown around her shoulders and she would cycle home, shouting the remains of our conversation back at me because her mind was never still— leaving me smiling at my good fortune at being her friend. She was an inspirational girl, and I felt honoured to be in her company, and to be her right hand on the rare occasions when this evidently made her life a bit easier (which, in truth, didn't seem very often).

We once had a fire in our school laboratory, where chemistry was our favourite lesson. Before our teacher—who was also the fire warden—had taken stock of what was occurring, Clem had located the extinguisher, broken the seal and pulled the pin; and was discharging the contents into the offending basin of flames. Although not the recommended course of action for one of the pupils, the teacher was clearly impressed, as Clem was invited to demonstrate her dexterity once again in front of the whole school in a subsequent assembly. Most of the students were transfixed by the sight of a fire that was ignited in their midst by an attendant marshal;

however, my eyes were trained only on Clem's exquisitely able, one-handed manoeuvre which, although now clearly practised and perfected for her star performance, had leapt out of her repertoire of physical abilities in the lab on the day of the real fire as instinctively as any one of the rest of us might have grabbed for a tissue to catch a sneeze.

In later life, I made another close friend. We were an unlikely pairing, Arthur Smith and I, as, on the face of it, we saw our worlds through completely different-coloured lenses; and he couldn't have been more different to Clem if he'd had two hands, horns, and a tail.

With no children of my own, and believing I could make a difference to a child in need, I had made an unsuccessful attempt to adopt a little boy called Torran whose family was struggling to look after him. It was during this process that I met Art, as he was the boy's grandfather: an old man who refused to remove his thick outdoor jacket, or stray too far from his seat by the door, in case he was asked to contribute more than simply being present.

Art came from another world (one in close but generally undiscovered proximity to my own), but I learned he had fathered a child in mine. He was the quiet member of Torran's family, leaving the talking to his brother-and-sisters-in-law who were Torran's great uncle and aunts. Art was a grandfather who didn't seem to support or disapprove of whoever might be adopting his grandson—until I was turned down. He asked me to accompany him, all the way to a place where our two worlds were riven yet connected, an unremarkable park bench where we could sit together and yet walk away into separate realities: mine the world of my laboratory and Torran with his new family, his a world of relative solitude with the works of a long-dead poet and philosopher called William Shakespeare. The discovery took my breath away, but for him it had long been known as a perfectly natural phenomenon—the plurality of human existence—and it seemed he'd chosen to move between his world and mine.

'*There are more things in heaven and earth, Rini, than are dreamt of in your philosophy.*' This was something he had borrowed from his poet. In his own words, he said: '*Rini, did you really think your world was the only one?*'

Once the reality of this had hit home, and I had dispelled what I had first thought might be the ruminations of a disappointed and bad-tempered old man, I learned that the society where Art came from was not as regulated as mine and Clem's, but it was a place where people with my skin colour or her apparent disability were often judged because of this outward difference between them and someone with a lighter skin tone or with all of their limbs intact. It seemed these people could, in some circumstances, still attain what was referred to in my world as governor status (and increasingly more so in the later stages of Art's lifetime), but there remained a stigma around this physical *inferiority*. It made me wonder how different life might have been for Clem and me, as children, if our families had not wanted us to play together because my skin was brown, and she occasionally needed help with threading a needle.

These are the types of things that I discuss with Art when we walk in the woods. We are a world apart, and yet connected (and I mean more so than the obvious link with his grandson). At his age, he has become accustomed to having his philosophies dismissed as fancy, or the onset of senility, and I am accustomed to believing no one is interested in the musings of Curators. But, for a time, our boots crack through the same undergrowth, and our coats repel the punctures of the same thorny branches on our woodland walks, and our worlds are united.

He refuses to wear the face mask that I tell him will protect him from catching or spreading the virus (that they're now calling *Virid20*), as he prefers to court Fate, and is disdainful about prolonging his life any longer than he would deem necessary. I remind him of my responsibility, nonetheless, not to let him carry it into his world where it could cause untold devastation (a vaccine still evades us despite the best efforts in our laboratories), and he briefly holds his tongue and ties a scarf around his face, like a bandit, to placate me.

I was turned down as Torran's adoptive parent on the grounds that they had found him a home with two parents who had other children: in short, a family. His grandfather favoured me: I had become his friend, which may have made him blind to the logic of this preferable settlement for his grandson. He is inclined to drink too much red wine, and rail against the world—both his and mine—and he was convinced I had been rejected because my skin was darker than Torran's. I think Art eventually came round to the fact that this wasn't the case, and it had been the more expedient decision for Torran at the time. The boy's life didn't go on to be as neatly resolved as the adoption committee might have anticipated when his file was closed, but I am more aware than most of the paradox of filing. As an archivist where I preside over row upon row of files, I know their contents usually only tell a partial truth, and often conclude nothing. However, a decision had to be made for Torran for better for worse, and who's to say a life with me would have turned out better for him? Sometimes 'it is what it is' (a phrase I learned from Art, that he subsequently despised!), and Torran and I have never lost touch with each other, which would always have been my intention, with or without a committee's blessing.

As for Clem, all those years ago, when the time came for the Decision to be made, she narrowly escaped what I believe would have been the wrong classification. She came from a family of Governors, and the expectation was set that she would follow in their footsteps. Her grades were usually good, and always enhanced by her fervent determination to do her best. She arrived late for one of our deciding exams because she had begun her day with a flat tyre on her bicycle, and neither of her parents was available to drive her into school. We assumed this would be taken into consideration (and, eventually, it was) but when our results were announced, she received an 'unclassified' grade for this exam which threw her overall marks into disarray. This caused much consternation within her family, and amongst the other families who knew her pedigree, and her parents mounted a challenge with the school's administration. At the same time and, possibly, under the same steam (as there was a growing tendency in our society to question such things), my father declared he was going to challenge *my* Decision too. I still grow hot with anxiety at the memory of his misguided mission, born out of his devotion to me—and maybe out of a modicum of paternal disappointment that his youngest child would not make the Governor grade of her more clever siblings.

I had never felt like Governor material, and felt uneasy and unhappy walking around school with teachers' eyes on me with a novel intensity that suggested I wasn't worthy of the challenge. They knew. I knew. I was glad when it was over. Clem was justly re-classified while I, Rini, was confirmed without any shadow of a doubt (or evidence to the contrary from my previous performance) as a solid candidate for curatorship. I knew this meant I would never be readily considered for a career that would allow for independent decision-making without the sanction of a Governor. It wasn't unheard of to prove one's change in worth at a later stage of career development, and to cross this divide, but it was unusual. When I recollected this to Art, he found it preposterous and described me as being afforded no more ambition, at best, than a freedman from his knowledge of 'slavery in ancient Rome', as opposed to a modern young woman with a world of opportunity at her disposal. He couldn't accept that I was content with my classification, and that I believed my disposition was better suited to social service than any form of governorship. When he was in a ranting mood (usually after half a bottle), and after I had borne witness to such a tirade or two, I began to suspect that his dissatisfaction was rooted, perhaps, in his own history, and the blurred lines that existed in his world between the value of a top university drop-out who was destined to run a shop (which was his own life's story), and someone who might otherwise have ended up, in his own words, as a 'mover and shaker'. I told him he had, one way or another, chosen the path of the Curator, and that there was no shame in that. He said that was bullshit, and he was probably better off dead anyway. Then, in general, he slept, and I would nurse his subsequent hangover with mint tea, and a few drops of a tincture I had come across at work that seemed to dissolve his headache and his bad mood—at least until the next one took hold.

I saw Clem recently with her baby daughter, beating her two little fists in the air from the confines of her pushchair like a testament to her flawless genes. Clem studied medicine, and became a birth defect specialist—although never able to conduct surgical procedures with her one, albeit highly efficient, hand. She was rushing to an appointment with baby Alba in tow, trying to talk nineteen-to-the-dozen sense from behind her anti-virus face mask. I couldn't make out her message until I got home to my computer, and read her subsequent email. She had found the letter I had written to our headmaster on the day she was late for our exam all those years ago. She said motherhood must have made her sentimental, as reading it again had made her cry. I had forgotten I'd written it: I just remembered feeling hollow with grief for my friend whose childhood ambition had always been to find a way, through scientific research, to grow back her missing arm and the arms of millions of others, and this ambition was now in jeopardy. The headmaster had handed it to her when he gave her the good news about her Decision. It was only now that she realised she had never said thank you. I found myself smiling in the guise of my younger self, basking again in the sheer joy of her friendship. We both knew my letter would have had no real bearing on the Decision, but maybe it was part of a bigger landscape of empowerment through support. If I weren't afraid he would turn it into a tiresome excuse to sing my praises, I would use this example to convince Art that it is sometimes more gloriously satisfying to thrive in the wings than it is to take your uncertain chances under the lights on the main stage. He would probably like the analogy, as it would remind him of Mr Shakespeare. I have reached the pinnacle of my life's ambition. I'm not sure Clem ever will.

I am not completely without sympathy or gratitude for Art's high opinion of me, however. It would be a strange state of affairs if people of two different generations from two separate worlds were to see eye to eye on everything, and I am not so humble that I don't admit to enjoying elements of his flattery. As he studied so much literature in his youth, he can quote poetry to prettify his praise, and to add weight to his arguments and wine-induced testimonials. Poets seem to be afforded more reverence in Art's world than in mine: it's not that their worth is unrecognised in my world, it is just not grounded in science, and therefore of significantly lesser importance. It is also unfair of me to present Art as a drunkard, as he has had a sizeable share of hardship in his life that would turn prouder men to the solace of wine and its anaesthetic properties to combat pain and stress. Since my first brush with death in dealing with Becks' poorly hamster, my life has been punctuated with tumours in one form or another. We grow them on unfortunate creatures in the laboratory in order to advance our knowledge of human medicine; and Art has had surgery to remove a tumour from his throat. My admittedly unschooled brain begs the question that, if we could better understand the reasons why things grow in our bodies in unwanted, and often deadly, ways, could we not develop the ability to grow welcome and beneficial ones, such as absent kidneys or (in Clem's case) missing limbs? It is this notion, perhaps, that makes my work at the university a little less sorrowful, and certainly more meaningful. It was that possibility that resided in Clem's brain all those years ago when she was determined to rebuild people, beginning with herself. Mercifully, she has been able to progress from some of the potential to the practical solutions of research, leaving the likes of me to line up her test tubes, swab her surfaces, and file her notes. I live in perpetual hope that any good that will come out of our research will outweigh the bad.

My closest colleagues at the university are called Tam and Dee. They are my only workplace companions at the moment, as the *Virid* restrictions mean we have to exist in social 'bubbles' with limited contact with the wider world. I am used to being surrounded by interesting people who occasionally tell me what I do is invaluable. Mostly, I update records and retrieve files for their work: nothing complicated, just time-consuming for minds that are trained on matters of a higher order than mine. My work is essential, but could be done by almost any other conscientious Curator who doesn't mind admin as well as working with the animals. I glean a lot of satisfaction out of being the last person to take stock of these creatures in this life before they begin their journey to the next. I look into the eyes of rabbits—as red as thermometer fluid—and rats, and mice, and wonder what they will become: maybe kings, queens, inventors (or their Curators like me). Who knows? I'm glad the mystery of their time on this earth and their new life in the next world remains just that: a mystery. And since I met Art, I believe there may well be a gateway to another world, even for the humble mouse.

Tam, Dee and I are accustomed to each other's way of doing things in the lab; and it's not so bad for me to see them—and only them—most days. I think Tam feels the same, although I'm not so sure about Dee. Tam is the best sort of Governor as he treats me like an equal, despite the obvious difference in station. When Dee isn't around he is happy to chat, and was particularly kind to me a few years ago when Ben left. Tam's gaze is deep and compassionate, and holds you like an embrace that he might never perform with his arms. Dee looks right through me as though I'm a sweeping brush that's been left out of the cupboard, in need of being stowed away again. Art is aghast when I tell him how life can be for the likes of me in my world, because there are rules where he comes from to prevent inequality at work. He doesn't accept that, for me, it's the natural order of things, and that it keeps our lives running smoothly and harmoniously. I don't resent Dee—I respect her for her superior abilities, and admire her graceful, gazelle-like demeanour—but I prefer the company of Tam. It's as simple as that.

'*Do you feel beautiful?*' Art once asked me, out of the blue. There was an interval of nervous laughter (mostly mine), and a change of subject which was easily managed, as he was in the habit of drawing my attention to things that were remarkable or uniquely beautiful (but never *me*, thankfully, up till then!) like tree fungus, or the iridescent wings of insects on the surface of a pond.

'*No!*'

'*Not even sometimes? Never?*'

'*No.*'

I do feel guilty when I take my walks with Art in his woods—our woods—because I am free of the constraints of a *Virid* world, unlike anyone else I know. Because of these, Torran is out of bounds, but does occasionally send me messages on his phone. I wish I could take him with me to sit in a café with his grandfather, or to see something amazing in this parallel universe, like a museum of ancient artefacts we have never seen, or unusual animals in captivity in the zoo. But Art forbids it. For all the complaints he makes about our worlds, mine and Torran's, he couldn't bear to release his grandson into his own without the confidence (or perhaps the belief that he has enough time left) to help him make sense of it. Perhaps we both underestimate the resilience of youth, and of this particular boy whom we both love, but we live in hope that a vaccine is on its way to open up his life experiences once again—a life in a world that at least he understands. He has never asked to see his grandfather's house. This is a blessing and a disappointment to Art in equal measure. I know Torran well enough to understand that he would never push on a door that he feared might be locked—he has suffered enough rejection in his life not to risk that— and he knows (in normal, non-*Virid* circumstances, of course) that my door, unlike his grandfather's, would always be open. I wouldn't undermine his adoptive parents' now legitimate claim on him, but I do wish Torran could forge a better connection with his grandfather, while he still can. Art has decided he is beyond this challenge, as he has spent too many years adrift from what he should call his family. He now expects me to help look out for him, and this comes as neither a surprise nor a hardship:

'You would have taken the best care of him, Rini. Shown him a better way of living.'

'I would have tried,' I said. *'But I'm not a family.'*

Art shakes his head and holds it between his hands.

'You're my family.'

He tells me Torran is receiving demerits for anti-social behaviour. I know these will count against him when he finally leaves school, and wants to apply for jobs. Always with an eye for a pretty face, Art modified his habitual recalcitrance towards the end of our family therapy sessions in order to make himself more amenable to the young woman who coordinated our appointments. He convinced her that it was in the boy's best interests to keep his frosty-turned-friendly grandfather informed of his ongoing welfare. He would make it his business to turn up (bandit scarf duly donned), and wait for her to finish work and, whenever she wasn't working, he would leave a note with the receptionist detailing when he would return. In the course of time, she reported that an older step-brother was proving to be the worst kind of role model, and that Torran was falling in with a bad lot: petty theft, an incident of shoplifting, verbal abuse of authorities, and his incrimination in stealing a car. Art called this latter pursuit 'joy-riding'—although we both suspected it wouldn't end up bringing much joy to either the owner of the car or its foolish young passenger. In pre-*Virid* times, I used to have the occasional cup of tea with Torran's mum, but lately we have lost touch and, of all things, being in any sort of trouble wasn't what he chose to mention in his increasingly unenlightening messages. I think of his brow—too furrowed for his tender years—knitting in pained concentration under his mop of unruly black hair as he punches, deletes, and punches again a dutiful line or two into his phone. I imagine the back of his grubby hand dragging away unwanted tears, as he strives to focus on the task. I remember days out with him when his longer-term life with me was still a possibility—days now relegated to our shared past—feeding ducks, and teaching him how to focus on fastening his anorak without catching his jumper in the teeth of his zip.

'Keep your train on the track', I used to tell him, and he would repeat these words to me whenever he saw me putting on my own jacket.

Art is morose about his grandson, and I know it is a mood steeped in guilt and self-pity. I would like to urge him to stay where he might be useful to the boy, but we both know there is no place in this world for a grandfather who has been such an infrequent and unreliable visitor. And my conscience would never allow this old man, who is also my dear friend, to put himself in the path of a virus that would lay waste to him as savagely as a spider decimating a crippled crane fly.

*

Gradually, the virus has taken its toll on the university. Although we knew it was coming and where the casualties were likely to cluster, we have been devastated by the loss of two of our most eminent professors, albeit (like Art) they had pre-existing conditions that put them in a high-risk group—one with his lungs, the other with a weakened immune system following treatment for cancer. They weren't young men. I give blood, probably more regularly than I should. Sometimes the people of the dispossessed community aren't well or numerous enough to provide theirs. I don't mind. If it helps the research into all the good work undertaken at my university, I am happy (and really quite proud) to help. Tam takes it ruefully, especially if it is more than once a week, in the unspoken knowledge we share that Governors like himself are never expected to donate blood or volunteer for any kind of drug treatment trials. It gives us quiet time together. He talks about his cat, Mademoiselle, whom he adores as if she were his child—habitually scolded yet forgiven for her many foibles, and praised beyond what she deserved for her rare acts of feline loyalty—and it doesn't seem to matter that I don't have too many interesting things to share with him about my life, *Virid* restrictions notwithstanding. It's enough that he talks, and I listen. I recognise in him some of the things I miss about Ben. When he is finding the spot on my arm for the point of his needle, I can see into the roots of his hair, greasy and flecked with tiny white dots of skin if he hasn't washed it for a while, but it has a vital, peppery scent that makes me feel safe and necessary.

It is a long time since I woke in the same bed as Ben, with his breath at my neck and his arms locked around mine. I have preserved in my consciousness moments of intense happiness in the same way that I have preserved the contents of my test tubes. I un-stopper them occasionally and remember warm bed sheets, windy beach walks with Lora's shrill little voice competing with the seagulls, chips and ice-cream, promises of a wedding on a cliff-top. He was my partner for four years, and I was a substitute mother for his daughter before I volunteered to care for Torran. Lora used to urge me to give her a baby sister, but she was at that whimsical age when the three of us lived together, when her imagination was as wild as her chatter, and she could have had no idea whether her fancies would translate into outcomes that would bring her true happiness. When I was her age, I wanted to live in a castle—at the very top, in a turret where only the most invested people would make the effort to climb up to visit me. It never came to pass, of course, which was just as well, as I think I would have led a very lonely life, rather than this life which has given me a purpose among purposeful people. Lora has grown to be clever, and is no doubt destined to be a Governor. She now lives with her reunited parents—Ben and his once estranged wife Demmy—and she has a little brother.

'You have lost everything you have ever loved.'

Art had drunk too much wine while I had barely managed one glass from the bottle.

'I think I've gained more than I've lost.'

My carefully sipped measure of alcohol had released a trickle of pleasure beneath the skin of my ribcage, while his hastily gulped glasses were simply making him more dissatisfied.

'We will die alone, Rini, you and I.'

There was a baby.

Demmy was Dee's twin sister, and she had an important job flying between continents, advising governments, which meant she couldn't be home as much as Ben in order to look after their daughter Lora. They needed help, so Dee recommended me, and introduced me to the family. Lora was challenging when her dad was around, but was much more amenable with me. Ben liked to come home from work (after I had finished at the university, and collected her from school) to find his daughter sitting at the tea table eating chickpeas and carrot sticks with clean fingers, rather than screaming at him and running away from their take-away dinner. He told me after a few months that Demmy had fallen in love with someone else in Geneva. He told me that part of his life, and Lora's, was over. Soon after that, he told me he was in love with me, and climbed into my bed. Then his bed became my bed.

I engineered the miscarriage of my secret child when I heard Demmy was on her way home. Ben had told me it would be a dinner—just a dinner— to talk through Lora's future, but his excitement was palpable, and it amazed me how the ties to his child's mother, despite everything, had remained so significant and so strong. He bought Lora a new dress, and told her she would be able to stay up late and eat with the grown-ups, which made her squeal with delight. Demmy returned, flame-haired and red-lipped, and her vivacity and her innate Governor's comportment reignited the fire of her family. Ben found unnecessary ways to try and explain, to apologise, but I understood— it was the natural order of things, brought back into order after a period of irregularity.

I knew enough about the chemicals at my disposal to bring about a death in my womb. I have a tiny reminder of my shot at a different life perfectly preserved and suspended in formalin in the laboratory at work, alongside several other specimens. I have moved the jars of foetuses around to make mine less remarkable, but, for me, I think she is destined to always stand out from the rest.

*

It has been an unusually warm spring and early summer. We are grateful for that, at least, as the lockdown has been a miserable clipping of our wings. I live in a flat with no garden of my own, but the communal gardens have been a godsend, even though the warden has been a bit of a bully, enforcing the 'two metre rule' with a ruler he has fashioned out of a length of cardboard painted an alarming, luminous green. His face— or as much of his face that we can see behind his mask—has become extra ruddy, as I suspect, like Art, he has been inclined to overindulge, wine-wise. He has taken it upon himself to reprimand the local children with short, sharp phrases to keep them mindful of the council's advice: his latest being, 'Face—Space—Chase', which has involved him running after them (if they aren't wearing their masks or keeping the prescribed distance from each other) in order to threaten them with his luminous lance. A few of them have started mounting a retaliation of, 'Fat—Flat—Twat', which, when I relay this to Art, makes him laugh like I have never seen him laugh before. It is an unfamiliar term of abuse to me, but is known in Art's world—which goes to show our worlds must cross over more than we have realised!

I think of Torran who is now sixteen, persuaded of similar rebellious notions that are bringing deeper consequences than a mere flick with a cardboard whip.

My brother, sister and I were never rebellious children. We could be naughty—Reggie vengeful, Becks spiteful, me goading them, perhaps, by my refusal to take sides—but we were united in our desire to please our parents who preached family harmony and conciliation at all times. Neither my mum nor my dad had brothers or sisters themselves, so they probably didn't understand the inevitably fractious nature of having to share everything in their younger lives with siblings. They were an unusual match: it wasn't unheard of for Governors and Curators to meet and marry (which is why I never dismissed the possibility of a life with Ben), but it was extraordinary enough for an architect (my mother) to marry a builder (my father). He was every bit her equal intellectually, claiming this as the result of loving—and learning from—her. For her part, she was convinced that he had been wrongly classified when his Decision was made, in an era when these things were rarely challenged. He was, however, a great builder. He built our house, and, to me, that made him a builder of dreams: ours, and many other families' to follow.

We lost them far too soon—when we were young adults—but, mercifully, they died together, at the wheel of their car. They collided with an oncoming articulated lorry, driven by a poor fellow who was neither drunk nor overtired: just, it seemed, confounded by a moment's loss of concentration that resulted in a lifetime of devastation. I never told my brother or sister that I met him several months after our parents' funeral. It wasn't necessary to tell them, and would have been unkind given their all-consuming bitterness and grief. His name was Joe Solomon—now abandoned by his wife—and was a man left, after a horrendous accident, to make unfixable amends for an innocent crime; every bit a victim of cruel circumstances as my mum and dad had been. It was good to meet him, and to tell him what my parents were like, and that they wouldn't have judged him harshly, and neither did I. He was glad of our meeting; and, by the end of it, he was able to talk about plans for his future. He said he didn't believe he would ever drive again, but had hopes of becoming a gardener. I think he walked away with a greater sense of purpose than when he arrived, his sunken shoulders drawn back, and his legs planting firmer footsteps behind the worn knees of his jeans.

Occasionally, I wake from a nap with my mother's or my father's voice sounding in my head—an exclamation, a rebuke, or just some words of love. It feels as though a cold hand has seized and squeezed my heart, and made it ache. Then I remember they are at peace, together, and I'm relieved that they will never have to endure the despair of old age, or the trauma of living through—or dying on account of—a pandemic, and I rest a little easier.

It has been harder for Reggie and Becks. All their lives they seem to have expected unconditional love, and this has evaded them.

*

Dee has heard she has been chosen to join the team researching the vaccine, and she is leaving the university. I will not be sorry to see her go; but am also pleased that her superior skills will be used to their best advantage. With her around less often, I feel liberated, as she used to hang over me when I was going about my filing duties, whilst being careless in her own efforts to return documents to where they belonged. It reminded me of Torran having to learn to put books back in my bookcase—except he was a child with co-ordination and concentration issues, not a grown woman at the peak of her governorship. I have wondered more than once about this tendency, which seems out-of-kilter with the rest of her. According to Tam, she is so punctilious at home that she cleans the grout between her bathroom floor tiles on her hands and knees with a toothbrush!

I am disappointed for Tam who must feel he was been overlooked, although he is full of praise and admiration for his colleague. He and Dee used to be lovers, so I assume this is the foundation for his generosity. For the final time, I message them both to tell them one of the rabbits has a tumour so large it is struggling to stand. The protocol is lethal injection by (or in the presence of) a Governor. I am happy to do it, as I have nurtured the rabbit from birth, and have monitored its growth and deterioration, but it must be witnessed and signed off. I'm glad it's Tam who comes, and he stays for a cup of tea; and we talk about something and nothing, least of all the absence of Dee who had promptly deemed her attendance at such a trivial act of administration a waste of her time. Our fingers curl round our mugs for warmth in the chilly kitchen; Tam is already in his winter sweater that is old and stretched into almost-holes from years of comfortable wear. We are suitably resigned that it will be just him and me now, at least until we see an end to the pandemic.

We have a champagne send-off for Dee, held in the smartest rooms at the university, with a buffet of canapés that, in pre-pandemic times, would have been handed round among us on silver plates by waiters; and she talks loudly about her new role in combatting *Virid20*. Her tone is solemn and precautionary, despite being the one—when the news was breaking—whose reaction over tea with Tam and me was that it was overblown, and unlikely to result in a significant infection of the population. However, we have all been living and learning, as the weeks and months of this invasion of our biology have been unfolding.

I haven't tasted champagne for years, and its effect on me is a feeling of pure contentment. I help with the clearing up when people have dispersed, and look out of the windows at the irrepressible influence of autumn on this late-summer evening: the street-lamps defying the fading natural light. Between the black railings of the university building, I see Tam turning up his collar around his lengthening hair to face a solitary walk home to Mademoiselle, who will no doubt be complaining for her dinner, and expecting compensation of sorts for the hours she's spent without him to do her bidding.

I anticipate that Art will be waiting for me, sat on the steps that lead up to my flat, indulging me, I hope, by wearing his scarf tied around his nose and mouth.

I wonder that no one has ever asked me where he came from or disappeared to. Foolishly, I used to think we might be invisible to people in our respective other worlds, but, I remembered, of course, that Art was a perfectly visible member of Torran's family therapy group, albeit a silent and grumpy one. I think the truth is that there is a tendency in both our worlds to see through people unless there is something we value in their presence. How else could I explain Dee's disregard of me? Art suggests the world (the universal one we share) is stocked with far too many self-serving individuals. It's no wonder to me that he holds this belief, and that he is what he is, given he can't remember ever being hugged as a child. Not once. His doctor seems convinced that his cancer is cured, and yet he is certain it will be back, biding its time to wreak inevitable revenge on him for real or imagined past misdemeanours. This conviction seems to be getting in the way of him living the rest of a meaningful life, not helped by the notion that it didn't have much meaning in the first place.

I feel blessed that *I* don't see through people; that I see Art and his grandson very clearly, as well as my brother and sister, Tam and Dee, and even poor Joe, who seems less poor the more I see of him.

ARTHUR (II)

The Boxing Day that I returned to Rini's world—many years before I met her there, and far too many since I had last visited my wife and daughter—began in an unextraordinary fashion with a walk in the woods accompanied by Steve and his spaniel Mindy.

Mindy was determined to make up for the previous day spent languishing by the festive oven—her sighs of frustration unheeded—by tearing through the undergrowth after her ball like she had been fired from a cannon.

More than once, we passed the park bench that had always been the marker of that ethereal boundary, and the one I had been rigorously avoiding for three decades. I found myself throwing Mindy's ball close by in the hope she might disappear after it, inviting Steve and I to follow her into this otherworld together as allies—but I was hoping in vain.

It wasn't until I returned later on my own that I found myself walking again through what used to be a familiar breach into the parallel universe that I had once, albeit briefly, considered might be my Brave New World. It seemed no one else was to be granted access—at least neither Steve nor Mindy that day—and I decided there was meaning in this: that my latest journey was one I was supposed to make on my own, as I had always done before; with no one else to express wonder, pass judgement, or to have my back should things not go as smoothly as they might.

The air was as crisp and refreshing as my memory of any woodland walk on a Boxing Day, which had always been a blessed childhood escape from the bothersome heat of my parents' house: a heat that usually kindled under a prickly new Christmas jumper, still impregnated with the odour of sprouts and burning goose fat despite its welcome baptism into the outdoors.

Now in middle age, I was nervous about what I might discover, and whom I might meet. There had been a time when my whole body felt alive and alert to new adventures—this might have explained my ability to stride, unchecked, into another existence. These days, I felt drained of any real enjoyment or ambition, and the opinion of an inconsequential woman over a Christmas dinner had possibly cut to the quick of my condition: that I had abandoned my responsibility as a husband and father, and would be forever in moral purgatory until I faced up to what I had done, and discovered what had befallen my family.

I was right to be nervous.

The aspect of the commune where I had briefly co-existed with Amber and our child appeared much brighter than I remembered—or it may just have been modernised over the years in a way that my own flat above a dowdy shop on a run-down street had not. The gardens were still neatly maintained, but showing more obvious signs of ownership, such as hand-painted names and numbers on their gates and sheds, that hadn't been the case before. The solitary figure of an old man was bent in service of his plot as I drew near, both of us observed by a nonchalant cat. I assumed, like me, he was either glad of a routine distraction from festivity, or had no one with whom to share it.

Amber lived at number seventy: a memory I hadn't acknowledged for years, despite still picking it out, when my hand was forced, as one of my significant numbers in a raffle or a lottery. She had made our own door sign one day out of a pair of wall tiles that she painted with little white flowers, while her baby was sleeping, and I, her husband, was stacking a bonfire with our neighbours. All these years later, it was still there, speckled with a few of the imperfections of age, next to a hook that was often hung with a basket of flowers and foliage. But not today. It was, after all, the middle of winter; although I noticed as I knocked on the door and stepped tentatively back, that most of the other houses were decorated with Christmas wreaths. Not hers.

I knocked again. There was a rumble and a thud from within, and the door was eventually opened by a bleary-eyed man, around my age, dressed in a dishevelled combination of pyjamas and daywear. The odour of stale fried food, cigarette smoke, and alcohol wafted my way like the stench of unsealing a tomb.

'I'm sorry to bother you,' I said.

Somewhere between finally closing my eyes on my resolve to embark on this mission the previous night and knocking on Amber's door that morning, I had made up my mind to throw caution to the wind, and just do it, without further planning or preamble. I had come unarmed, with neither gifts nor festive treats, and—judging by the state of the man at the door—that decision now seemed vindicated.

'I'm looking for Amber?'

'I'm Archie,' said the current inhabitant of Amber's house. His eyes searched me from head to toe for evidence of the reason for my visit . 'It will be for me.'

'I don't have anything,' I said. 'I used to live here, years ago, with Amber and our daughter Angelica.'

'She's dead,' he said, rubbing his unshaven chin with uneasy dismay. 'And she's not here anymore. The daughter, I mean..' He saw my expression which must have been sobering. 'I'm sorry. Amber died a couple of years ago. And the kid was a problem. She's been put away.'

A strange quandary of emotion shivered through me, as I took stock of my bearer of bad news. He looked like he was about to sink to his knees with the effort of answering the door and my questions.

'Can I come in?' I asked, thinking on my feet. 'Do you have a kettle I can use to make us a drink?'

Later, I realised he'd thought I was bringing him drugs or medication, or both. He stepped aside, succumbing to both my request and his obvious disappointment.

I found the kettle and two mugs that were cracked but clean, and a jar of coffee that was so old I was required to dig the granules out with a sharp teaspoon.

'Do you live here alone?' I ventured, to restoke the conversation.

'Oh, yeah,' he said. 'Now that Amber's gone. It's been hard. It was hard for both of us.'

He took my offering of black coffee, served in what I assumed was one of his own cups, into a shaky, two-handed grip.

'What happened?' I asked. 'You must forgive me; it's been such a long time since I visited. I knew Amber twenty-five years ago.'

'Her husband left her,' he said, clearly having not processed the earlier part of our discourse. 'With a kid and everything. This place is alright, but they didn't want her living here on her own, so they moved me in.'

'Moved you in?'

'Yes, you know how it is.' He eyed me as though he was only slightly unsure I might not 'They decided we would do well together, neither of us having anyone, and me being good with fixing things, and being out of the facility with nowhere to go.'

'The facility?'

'I was put away for drugs stuff,' he said, by way of reply. He kept trying to take a draught of his coffee, but it remained too hot, and his suction too unreliable, to let him succeed. He put down his mug, and hunted instead through his dressing gown pockets for a part-smoked cigarette. Instinctively, I picked up his lighter and ignited the ragged tobacco with my steadier hand.

'But you were back on the straight and narrow?'

'You know how it is,' he said again, with continuing confidence in my knowledge of how his life (and that of my wife and daughter) had been. 'Everybody means well. Dillan is a good bloke, but he's never had a habit. Me and Amber did what we could, but it was always a battle, and the kid was never right in the head. I used to tell Amber Dillan was right, she had to let her go. She did in the end but she wa'n't happy about it.'

'Where did Angelica go?' I dared myself to press. He was now leaning forward, successfully slurping his hot coffee. Mine remained untouched, like a bribe, on the table between us. 'Did she go to live with Dillan and his family?'

'What?' he said, his face contorting with the pain of confusion. 'Nah, he put her away, where she wouldn't get into any more trouble. She was a nice kid, good-looking too, which was maybe why she got knocked up so young. But not right in the head. Dillan took care of all that.'

His words were bordering on the unbearable, and I was about to raise my hand to ask him to stop, when there was a knock on the door: his second—and judging by the excitement of his reaction, much more welcome—Boxing Day visitor. He locked bloodshot eyes with me, as though he expected, and trusted, me to answer the door.

A young chap in a casual black uniform of zipped bomber jacket and sunglasses was on the doorstep—as jovially cavalier as any festive delivery man—with a brown paper bag.

'For Archie Whatton,' he said, as he handed his goods over to me. 'There you go. Merry Christmas.'

We opened the package on the kitchen table. There was a bottle of green liquid and a box of pills. I surveyed Archie's spoils with the sense that this was a regular and keenly anticipated drop.

My heart had started to drub in my throat. In my head, I was charging through the woods, screaming at the top of my lungs, stopping only to box a tolerant tree trunk with the balled fists of frustration. I wanted to run.

But I stayed.

'Would you do the honours, mate?' Archie said.

I took note of the sticky dark green circles on the table where he had made previous clumsy attempts at serving himself his precious concoction. The bottle came with a plastic measuring cup, so I duly poured his prescribed dose, and watched him knock it back with the accuracy of the addict who can find precision of purpose when desperate needs must.

For my own part, I took my fishing flask of whisky from inside my coat and took a swig. Both Archie and I seemed to need our respective shots to make it through the dilemma of this Boxing Day, for our different but fatally entwined reasons.

'I am grateful to you for you letting me in,' I said.

'It's all the same to me,' he replied, as he waited for his drug to take effect. 'Who did you say you were again? You were asking about Angelica?'

'Yes. I want to see her. You know how it is.'

'I doubt they'll let you in, unless you're a relative. Depends. Are you a Governor?'

'I'm a shopkeeper.'

'Ah. You might do better going through Dillan. He's retired now, but he will still have influence.'

'And Amber,' I said. 'How did she die?'

47

'We overdosed,' Archie said, serenely. 'She never recovered. I was the lucky one, if you call it luck. It was before things were regulated. S'different now.'

'So, you live here, instead of in the… facility, Archie?'

'What do you mean?' he said, without aggression. 'I did my time. I'm no criminal. The facility is no place for me anymore. Gelly was only put away for her own good. They would have found her a place here if she could have looked after herself. Maybe they'll let her back when she's a bit straighter. But she'd got caught up in the same shit as her mother and me. And a girl like that can't keep having babies, something needed to be done.'

'What happened to her baby?'

'She lost it.' Archie's eyes had been shut, but opened briefly and rolled sympathetically at the memory. 'Poor kid, she was beside herself, and so was her mother. Apparently there was absolutely nothing wrong with it as far as they could tell.'

'So Angelica, Gelly, where will I find her?'

'She's in one of the units,' he replied with a sleepy shrug. 'She'll be OK, she'll be well looked after. She's paid her dues. They took her eggs. She may not have had a kid of her own, but at least someone will. Maybe a ton of 'em.'

'Why would they take her eggs?' I found myself saying in miserable disbelief.

'To pay for everything, o'course. Amber always said her problems weren't genetic, so her eggs were valuable.'

'How did Amber know that?'

I took another swig of my whisky to assuage my growing anxiety.

'Dillan said. He was a baby doctor.'

'I remember,' I said, bitterly.

I had been trying to give up smoking. I'd toyed with the idea of it being my New Year resolution, so I still had a few days' grace. I decided to rifle through Archie's various coat pockets, hanging in the back lobby of the little house, and was rewarded by finding a crushed but partially stocked packet of cigarettes, and helped myself to one of them. I lit and smoked it hastily, angrily, in the yard, sucking the guts out of it as though it might give me strength. I returned to find him looking refreshed, attempting to make himself another cup of coffee. He had colour in his cheeks, and he looked younger than I had first perceived: he was probably several years younger than either Amber or myself. Years of substance abuse had taken their toll, but the magic green brew had restored the mask of his misspent youth, albeit perhaps for just the next few hours.

'Could you eat?' he asked me. I wasn't sure whether this was an invitation to cook or to be offered a meal at the grimy stove where I used to make omelettes, and bacon and eggs, with my young wife.

'No, thank you. I should be going.'

'Did you get what you came for?' he asked with lame innocence, as though he were in the habit of trading favours. He shivered a little, with his hands thrust under his armpits. 'You knew the family, right?'

'Yes, a long time ago,' I replied. 'There is one last thing. Do you have an address for Dillan? I don't think I have it anymore.'

Later that evening, I eschewed a cosy visit to my local pub with its open fire, and no-questions-asked camaraderie, and opted instead to take a trip to what my mother used to call the 'seedy' end of town, to remind myself of some of the haunts of my youth. Archie Whatton's tales of the fate of my wife and daughter had (as I no doubt expected they would) reawakened the abiding sense of guilt that had run through my adulthood like the vein through ancient marble that no amount of polishing could eradicate. But I could have had no idea how tragically Amber's and Angelica's lives would turn out: how the innocent commune that had seemed to me to be impervious to social decline would harbour the means to their destruction rather than provide them with a lifetime of relative peace without me. As I tramped home, I began to try and exonerate myself (to some small, pathetic degree) by reflecting on what more I could have done. What if I had stayed with them, would their lives (our lives) have turned out so much different? Maybe a girl like Amber was always going to fall foul of a weak resolve, such as the one that allowed her to drop her knickers so readily in the woods for a layabout like me? Maybe the product of such careless youthful copulation like Angelica was never going to amount to much more than becoming the victim of teenage pregnancy herself? I wandered past the drunks and drug addicts on my side of the tracks, and told myself things weren't so bad in this other land where I had taken leave of them, where society seemed to offer its underclass some kind of sanctuary, with regulated care facilities, and an organised, controlled prescription management regime, which the poor buggers who lay in some of the doorways in my world were denied.

I told myself.

But I didn't listen to myself for long.

My daughter had paid for her misdemeanours (and how could these not be mine, too?) by having her body violated, and with it perhaps her potential to have a child of her own taken away from her. Harvesting the eggs of young women of questionable mental health was something I could only ever imagine taking place in the Nazi Germany of the 1930s, which I knew was unheard of in Amber's world. I decided I should bide my time a little longer, gather my troubled thoughts, and make another visit: this time to see my former brother-in-law Dillan to seek some answers.

*

It wasn't until the spring of the following year that I felt strong enough to go back. My resolve would steel itself then weaken like a falconer's hand flexing inside its glove, unsure whether it had the confidence to meddle with the force of nature.

Archie Whatton had torn a page out of an old address book, and handed it over as meekly as giving up a bus ticket—having either no further need of Amber's brother's address, or possibly knowing it off by heart. Somehow I suspected it was the former not the latter. It was in Amber's handwriting—a childlike, girlish script with the downward curves of the letters embellished like the spirals of a snail shell. There was a telephone number, but I realised I had never used a telephone in Amber's world, and, in any case, I felt I ought to show up unannounced in person in order to guarantee an audience with what I remembered was a busy man.

I was unfamiliar with the district where Dillan lived, having never ventured far from the commune, or the woodland where I had briefly resided with his sister. I asked for directions on the street, and was given a travel route that I initially found confusing until I worked out it was simply a series of changes of public transport: green to Park (a bus ride); red to Anderson (a train ride) and then yellow to Mansion Gate (a pedestrian walkway). Remarkably, the currency in my wallet was almost identical to that of my fellow travellers—give or take the odd note that should have been a coin, and vice versa—but any discrepancy didn't give rise to questions, or impede my ability to take a seat on both the bus and the train, and head for my destination, which was Apartment Six, Hester House, Hester Way, Mansion Gate.

I found myself in an area not dissimilar to a smart postcode in London, clearly populated by those who took their money away from the hustle and bustle of the city, and enjoyed suburban living in smart houses on tree-lined streets and avenues. Hester House was no exception: a bright, tall building made of huge blocks of white stone, looming like a temple behind an imposing iron gate that would only to be penetrated with a degree of difficulty, or guile, by a seemingly random passer-by such as myself that day. The gatekeeper who responded to my press of the buzzer was predictably curt—'Who was I, where was I from, who was expecting me?'

I decided there was nothing to be gained from not simply telling the truth. My name was Arthur Smith, I was Dillan Archer's brother-in-law, and I wanted to see him.

'Is Mr Archer expecting you?' was the obvious next hurdle.

'No, but I'm sure he will see me,' I ventured.

'One moment,' came the reply. The gatekeeper eyed me over the top of his spectacles, as he talked officiously into his intercom. 'Your name again?'

I repeated my name, and imagined the confusion and potential resentment that the mention of it, after all these years, might be stirring behind the smart sash windows of apartment number six.

'Wait there,' said the gatekeeper, who proceeded to ignore me for the several minutes it took for the main door of the apartment building to open, and for Dillan to come through it and stroll without urgency to the gatehouse. I heard him say something like, 'Don't worry, Jensen, he's perfectly safe', to the gatekeeper, and approach the gate, where I was to remain on the other side like a prisoner granted a rare audience with his disinterested defence lawyer.

We surveyed each other for a moment, taking separate stock of how the past twenty odd years had changed us for better or worse—he, leaner, with shorter thinning hair, but displaying the general demeanour of someone who had lived a healthy, wealthy existence; me, decidedly bulkier in my habitual battered wax jacket, sporting the same collar-length, wilfully wavy hair that seemed to be getting more voluminous the greyer it became.

The last time I had spoken to him he had offered me a job as a librarian before I disappeared from his sister's life for good. Silently we acknowledged each other's identity, and then he said:

'The runaway returns.'

I began to babble. 'I was young and careless. I regret abandoning your sister like I did, but it was a long time ago.'

'Do you know she is dead?'

'Yes, I heard.'

'So what brings you here now?' Dillan shook his head in disbelief. 'Where exactly did you disappear to?'

'My parents didn't know about my circumstances. When they found out they threatened to disown me. I made a rash decision, and I've regretted it. Truly.'

The words that spilled out of me were a passable version of the truth. I had no desire to embellish it, yet was glad of the heavy railings that separated me from this man who had intimidated me in my youth, and was eliciting a similar reaction in middle age. My behaviour had been inexcusable, plain and simple.

'There's much to regret. Your daughter needed specialist care that Amber wasn't able to give her. She had a type of personality disorder that made living with her very challenging. She couldn't play or learn alongside other children. She couldn't concentrate, and was prone to having violent outbursts. With you gone, Arthur, they were vulnerable.'

'So vulnerable that someone thought the answer was to move a junkie criminal in with them?'

I gripped the railings for support. Amber's brother reached out and gripped them higher up, and more aggressively.

'Archie Whatton was a piece of shit. I had nothing to do with that decision,' he said, recovering his composure. 'But in the *real world,* it's what goes on. Communes don't run themselves, no matter how they might seem to occasional visitors like yourself.'

'Can you tell me where Angelica is? I want to see her.'

'I could give you her address, but I can tell you she won't want to see *you.* She doesn't want to see many people, and those she does usually end up on the wrong end of her temper. We're hoping she might be released back into the commune at some point, but she has a way to go.'

I remembered a small child without a care in the world who had her mother's dark hair and my weak mouth that was all soft lips and tiny chin, and whose only words ever spoken to me had been the repetition of *Dadda.* It was strange and uncomfortable to think of her as a grown woman with mental health issues: a lost baby, a lost life. My lost child.

'She had a miscarriage,' I said. 'That must have been dreadful for her, being so young.'

'You know a great deal these days,' said her uncle.

'I also know she has had her eggs harvested,' I continued, bravely.

Dillan frowned, as though his instinct was to distrust the man in his midst, for all sorts of reasons.

'Nothing out of the ordinary,' he said, assessing me as someone he was finding increasingly extraordinary. 'Standard procedure to finance her care—since her *father* was unable to make provision.' He eyed me dispassionately. 'Thankfully, people will pay well for the chance to have a child of their own. And your daughter may be dispossessed, but, like a lot of young women like her, she has been able to pay her debt to society. Tell me, how do you pay yours?'

'I work,' I said, defensively. 'I've always worked. I imagined, I hoped, that Amber would have friends in the commune who would look out for her—maybe even find a more worthy husband than me.'

'You mean you abdicated responsibility without really worrying about anyone but yourself,' said Dillan. 'Until now?'

I resisted hanging my head, but it was starting to feel like a possibility.

'I know you've tried to do right by Amber,' I said. 'And by our daughter. But do you really think she won't want to see her father?'

'She may well want to see you for the pleasure of spitting in your face, like she does to her uncle and aunts,' he replied with some humour. 'I can certainly tell her you have enquired after her well-being. Do you have a number, or an address, I can pass on?'

'I don't live here anymore,' I said. 'I live a long way away. It's hard to explain. If I thought you would understand, I would ask you to let me through these bloody great gates so I could try.'

'I see,' he said. 'You're still a man who comes with complications. I don't think you've been in one of the prison facilities, have you, or I would have known? Someone would have let it slip.'

'Do you remember the forest where we first met?' I said, suddenly. 'Where you brought Amber, to *ambush* me all those years ago?'

'I can visualise it, yes, just about. It's striding distance from the commune.' Dillan was a clever man: his face was working as though he were conjuring the coordinates in his mind's eye. 'Don't tell me *that's* where you live?'

'Strange as it may sound to you, I do, near enough,' I said. 'You might not remember, but there is a wooden bench—you don't have to look too hard if you know what you're looking for. I'm often there. Leave me a message, when you can. Let me know when you've seen her and ask her if I can visit. Would you please do that for me?'

'Are you on the run?'

'No,' I said. 'I'm not asking you to compromise your reputation, Dillan. But it's the only reliable way I can think of to keep in touch.'

'What do you expect me to do? Leave you a note pinned to a tree?!'

'Better if you stick it under the bench,' I replied, earnestly. 'I will check it every week.'

'You're an odd-ball,' he said, but not unkindly. 'I guess I shouldn't be surprised that my odd-ball sister found you so appealing. You haven't told me why you have turned up again after all these years?'

'It was something somebody said over a Christmas dinner,' I said. 'So I went back to the commune in the hope I might make peace with my wife and daughter. Instead I found Archie Whatton.'

'So he was the one who filled you in with your lost history,' he said. 'Did you have some sympathy for the evil little rat?'

'He is an addict,' I said. 'How could I not have some sympathy? Can *you* not?'

Dillan brought his face closer to mine at the gate.

'There was talk that he was the father of Angelica's baby,' he said, his jaw clenching on his words. 'There was no proof, of course, and she wasn't for telling. So I suggest your sympathy is misplaced. He was found dead in the commune earlier this year with a needle in his neck. It couldn't have happened soon enough.'

*

The weeks that followed my meeting with Dillan dragged like I was waiting for a glacier to melt to reveal a new landscape. I waited and waited. I took root on my bench in the forest, committing the sight of the trees before me to memory, until darkness fell, and I was obliged to stagger home. I felt they were staring pityingly back at me, willing me to become one of them, challenging the pointlessness of my human existence which was, it seemed, a state of perpetual expectation for something to happen that never would.

I checked under the bench on a daily basis, grasping at its splintered underbelly for evidence of communication—an envelope, a folded piece of paper. There was nothing.

I began to question whether Dillan would be able to access the bench from his side of our fractured universe, but I was convinced it was the marker of the divide, belonging in both his world and mine, and it should have been perfectly possible—with no further knowledge required—for him to find it if he put his mind to it, and if he remembered the woodland well enough, as he had suggested he did.

He had always seemed a man of his word. Why was he letting me down? I could understand his lack of commitment to my peace of mind, after all these years of abandonment, but I had more faith in him doing right by Angelica.

I practised composure, and reason; and began to visit less frequently. I imagined him going to see her on my behalf, getting spat at or worse, and returning to the comfort of his normal family with nothing to tell me.

I wondered whether I should go back to see him, and demand her whereabouts; and simply face her myself. I wrestled with my fear of her rejection, and the consequences of my self-loathing if she reacted badly to me turning up out of the blue.

I kept up my daytime vigil for the best part of six months. One day, someone turned up from the Forestry Commission and cut down a tree—one that was right in my eyeline—and began the task of sawing it into logs. It gave me a sense of both pain and pleasure: the former because the tree was among those that had begun to feel like tacit companions, supporting me in my endeavour; the latter because the chore was neatly and expediently performed by an expert chap who seemed to have no idea he was being watched.

The tree felling became symbolic. If something so ancient and mighty could be taken down in what still seemed to me to be its prime, how could a mere mortal like me, whose life had been characterised by weakness, do more than accept his fate as a failure?

I headed for home, but not before I had made myself known to the woodsman, and had shaken his hand. He was fleetingly perplexed by my interest, then we took our leave of each other.

I returned at intervals; and the tortuous days and weeks became easier, elastic months, and then years. Most of the trees remained the same, defying both the axeman and the less predictable strike of the lightning blade. The bench continued to stand its test of time as that unremarkable threshold to otherness for anyone like me, who might have possessed the true desire to seek it, and therefore be transported somewhere else.

I lost hope of ever hearing from Dillan or my daughter again. My life became a series of days done, punctuated by coffee in the morning to bring me round, and an excess of alcohol in the evening to tranquilise me to the sleep that I often hoped I wouldn't wake up from. I stopped being a shopkeeper, and left the flat above the ironmongers that had been my family home—or, at least, the space I had inhabited with my parents— since I was born. I moved to a small, mid-terrace house with an uninviting front door that was mostly toughened, opaque glass, and a back door that was only accessible through a six-foot wooden, padlocked gate. Steve's friends, David and Seth, took on the ironmongers, and made it modern and inviting, and, by the time the new century was underway, were offering floral gardening gloves and scented candles as well as hammers, nails, and power drills. I wondered if my parents would be turning in their graves at this development; and it was something that occasionally induced an inner smile in the moments before my curmudgeonly features crumpled in repose.

Then I got diagnosed with throat cancer.

I had barked, quite literally, at an irksome child in the launderette who had tripped over my bag of washing in pursuit of a toy rabbit: the offending article being repeatedly thrown up in the air and caught (or not) by its irritatingly persistent young owner. She had turned to her mother and said, 'That man sounds just like Grandad', whilst looking at me with round eyes that classified me as an alien, and a deaf one at that. We managed to ignore each other, and the pesky rabbit, until they were ready to leave, when the mother touched my elbow, and said, 'If you don't mind my saying, you should get your voice checked out. My dad has been poorly, but he's doing OK now.'

My experience of sentences that started with, 'If you don't mind my saying,' was usually to mind little enough to ignore how they ended. However, in a providential change to a habit of a lifetime, I took heed of two women and a flopsy bunny, and visited my doctor.

I had quit smoking years before, but I always believed there would be a day of reckoning for me, after years of less than exemplary living.

Something was going to be targeted, for sure. In terms of my genes, it was my father's heart and my mother's brain. I imagined for me it would be my lungs or my genitals, so the fact that it was my throat provided a cunning twist to my tale.

My life had been a series of obsessions—in no particular order: stars, trees, books, girls, hawks, fags, booze, drugs; then there was finding Angelica, my poor wretched child who was my only connection to my own humanity. Now there was battling cancer.

There would be more obsessions to come—Rini being the most life-affirming—but my illness was, for a time, all-consuming. Noley used to tell me I was 'a confounded nuisance', and she wasn't far from the mark, because, for someone who gave the impression to the world that he didn't care if he lived or died, I was prepared to throw everything I had at beating cancer. I had never been afraid of dying, but on my own terms. I had no intention of being killed by a stranger. Chemotherapy was grim, resulting in unmentionable bowel problems, sickness, and hair loss, but I convinced myself I was ushering in a type of foul yet disciplined task force that might be fighting dirty, but was intent on vanquishing an even dirtier, more dangerous foe.

I was eventually given the all-clear which, as any of the fellow survivors that I met at the clinic, or on the hospital ward, would attest, was more of a stay of execution than carte-blanche to skip off into a carefree future. I knew the rest of my life would be, at best, a series of check-ups that I would attend with bated breath, thanking my lucky stars until the next one, which would gradually get further and further away until I was old enough that no one would much care about the invitation to attend, or the outcome if I didn't.

Steve remained my only friend of note. He visited me when I was incapacitated, and drove me to my appointments. He lived with an amenable chap called Mark and (more importantly to me) a spaniel called Mabel who had replaced Mindy the second, the latter having chased her last imaginary pheasant into the gloom—her racing heart snuffed out like a little candle, used to burning at both ends that had met suddenly and fatally in the middle. It was the closest to tears that I had ever seen the man whom Noley and I used to refer to as 'quiet Steve'. He was certainly more quiet than usual for a while. Then, one night in the pub, Mabel appeared from inside his coat, looking for all the world like a tiny, fluffy-eared reincarnation of her predecessor, fashioned, perhaps, out of the balls of Mindy's fur we accumulated whenever we'd brushed out her lugs; and we were all a little smitten. Mark moved in soon after with a couple of proud cats that were tolerated rather than welcomed by both Steve and Mabel, which may have explained why Mabel was equally happy to spend the occasional night on my kitchen floor rather than on her master's, and why I began to think of myself as her co-owner. I guess it isn't in my nature to offer total commitment to anyone or anything, whether it be wife, child, partner, goshawk, or dog, but Mabel came as close to capturing my heart (the rigid, empty vessel that it seemed) as any mortal creature could.

As my particular fate would have it, it was Mabel who eventually brought me news of my daughter. I was laid up in bed with a debilitating flu-type bug that had probably taken advantage of my weakened state, when Steve and Mabel came by with a flask of Mark's obnoxious herbal tea and a scruffy, mud-stained envelope bearing my name. They had been out walking in the woods; and, rather than returning with her ball, and the smug spaniel demeanour of successful retrieval, Mabel had reappeared with a mouthful of paper that she sheepishly surrendered into Steve's grasp, and that he was now surrendering into mine. She put her head sorrowfully under the hand that dangled over the side of my bed, as though she thought she might be in trouble for puncturing the letter with her teeth marks and dropping it in the dirt; so I made a fuss of her, and passed it off as the prank of local children (convincing Steve that it had happened before). They soon left me in peace.

I was glad that Steve was as incurious about the content of the note that day as he had been on finding it the day before.

It was from Dillan, dated recently. Some twenty years I had waited without any encouragement of contact: so long that I registered his signature with such resentment I could almost have thrown his letter, unread, onto the fire. Almost.

To Arthur

I trust this letter will reach you as previous ones have not – and you have denied me any other means of communication.

My niece, your daughter, has been moved back into a secure unit where she will pose no more threat to herself or her son. Torran is currently living in foster care, but his longer-term situation needs to be resolved. If you still want to help your family (none of us are young men and women anymore), you can find us at the address enclosed. We meet on Wednesday mornings.

Dillan.

My infection had made me weak, possibly a little delirious, and I fell asleep after I had read Mabel's grubby victory note. I dreamed of the unfolding of the years since I had met a quirky young woman with black hair and a gap in her smile in the woods. I saw again our round-faced baby, laughing up at me from her crib, until her laughing mouth became a scream of rage, silenced only by the sweeping slap of a dark hand— maybe Archie Whatton's, maybe even my own. Then there was a boy, watching me in the woods, shadowy but persistent, appearing at every turn, as I tried to take a different course from my nightmare.

I was dreaming of my grandson.

DEE (I)

There are few things more energising than clearing clutter—even if it hadn't felt like clutter before—and I do this with great relish before I leave town to take up my new post.

For the hundredth, maybe thousandth, time in my life, I empty my drawers and cupboards, and discard what is no longer useful or desirable; and castigate myself for having spared so much of what should have been jettisoned before.

There is a headscarf that was a gift from an old boyfriend; and a scrapbook from my schooldays which, frankly, was more the work of my twin sister Demmy than mine. These are the first things to go. Demmy used to take delight in reminding me of my failings which was why the scrapbook had included our handwritten responses to a teacher's question, 'If you could wish for anything for Christmas, what would it be?': hers being 'World Peace', and mine 'To beat my sister at everything'. This had caused much mirth at school and at home—and I *eventually* saw the funny side—but I knew in my heart that it was the truth. As was my clever sister's cynical desire to be recognised as the supreme arbiter of the peace that she so innocently claimed she sought.

We were always the best of friends and the fiercest of competitors. Our parents decided to add to their family late in life as, sadly, our firstborn sibling had died in childhood, while our older sister was blind. Cassie is an excellent musician—a harpist—and governs her own school of music; but our parents, who were both successful doctors, were hopeful that they might produce offspring that would turn out to be more in their own image. My mother was a healthy and active woman late into her fertile years, and, having screened out a number of questionable foetuses, was impregnated with my sister and me, and so we were practically programmed from conception not to disappoint. As we grew, we learned to accompany our sister on the piano and violin; and studied hard to achieve bright careers in medicine like our parents before us.

My chosen field became virology, as I loved research, and was fascinated by the germ population that was so much more comprehensible to me than any human one. My sister thrived in general practice, and was a bold, clear communicator who eventually rose through the ranks of field medicine into something more strategic. She ended up knowing everything about my projects while keeping the finer details of her own work (understandably, I'm bound to admit) rather close to her chest.

As time went by, I realised I was never going to beat her at anything much at all, except the occasional game of Boardwords at Christmas; and, even then, our sister Cassie could hold her own against me, as we had the version that consisted of little yellow tiles embossed in the fingertip language of the blind. I often wondered why I even bothered turning up to her concerts, in a designer dress (one of half a dozen I would have ordered, tried on, and rejected because the buttons were too sharp, or the neckline wasn't right) to sit between Demmy's clever husband Ben and Cassie's handsome husband Kit, while their respective wives were either on an important mission overseas or holding an audience in thrall to her extraordinary talent. But this was my family, and I needed to fit in; and I had few friends, apart from them, to speak of.

I began my career working at a laboratory that was under the governorship of a Professor Whatton. He had a reputation for being dry and strict, which suited me well enough, as I knew where I stood with my assignments, and was not one for fraternising with my colleagues. I had been in the job for about nine months, and was comfortably in my stride with my routines and responsibilities, when there was an incident. It seemed that a number of my co-workers had conspired to produce a recreational drug on the premises that they eventually decided to try out on themselves with rather disastrous consequences. How they had found the inclination, the time, or the resources was beyond me; as was the ability to have forged such a close-knit, conspiratorial relationship with each other, either in work or outside of it.

Two of them experienced a terrifying trip which resulted in attempted suicide by jumping out of windows, whilst the remainder suffered panic attacks and fits. This was described to me in somewhat sketchy detail by the professor on a Monday morning in his office that was next to our laboratory. We were wearing our protective glasses, but he had removed his, seemingly to emphasise his great personal disappointment and dissatisfaction with the team. I remember feeling altered by the news, not least by the sense of isolation that (surprise, surprise!) I hadn't been included in their conspiracy, but, on another level, elated that I hadn't been a source of disappointment, and therefore both morally and professionally superior.

He said something vague about a personal family history of dishonourable death from drug addiction, and then went on to insist that I should not speak of this to anyone outside of the lab. I was offended by the suggestion that I might, but gave him my assurance, and quickly left this uncomfortable conference.

For the next few weeks, it was just the professor and me (plus one or two unnoteworthy laboratory assistants), and I felt a strange pressure building that had nothing to do with my work.

I usually went straight home to eat after work, but my days were suddenly so quiet and solitary that I decided to make a detour to the local café for my supper, and the company of strangers. It was an uneasy trade-off for me, as I was compromising my routine of a set menu according to what day of the week it was; but it seemed like a necessary thing to do for my mental hygiene. The café proprietor was a rotund man called Luigi who was amenable to my requests to serve his lasagne with the pasta on the side, or pizza with some of the toppings removed, although he would smile and say something unintelligibly sardonic under his breath about it, as he applied himself to wiping down his counter.

My father and my sisters called round, but I could scarcely pass the time of day, in case I let slip something about *the incident*.

Eventually, my co-workers returned: even the two who had injured themselves, and it seemed we were expected to continue as before, as if nothing had happened. In ordinary circumstances, the re-establishment of routine would have been a cause of satisfaction to me, but, in this case, I found it unsettling. At first, it was mild displeasure, as no one seemed to have been held to account—at least not visibly enough for my comprehension of it—and then it escalated into something more upsetting. I had stopped visiting the café after work, but had failed to fall back into organising my evening meals and my breakfasts. Subsequently, I was often hungry and out of sorts at work. The only way to remedy this, I decided, was to take my *lunch* break at the café, and to make this my main meal of the day—suboptimal as this change to my former habit felt.

The café was less busy during the day, and occasionally it was just me with Luigi presiding over my lunch plate and coffee cup. He expected to talk to me about his family, and for me to show interest in sentences punctuated with words like *'rigatoni'* and *'bambini'*. He wondered about the origin of my surname, which was as inconsequential to me as my ancestors' shoe-sizes. It seemed I had escaped the solitude of my workplace only to be held captive by a pasta chef. He wanted me to engage in conversation: What did I do? Where did I work? In spite of myself, I began to try to explain, as I was reliant on an intake of tuna fish and egg salad from his lunch menu to get me through the rest of my day. He listened intently, I thought, as I accounted for myself as best I could, given I wasn't in the habit of regaling myself to anyone, let alone an insignificant purveyor of café cuisine.

I was ready to finish and leave one day, when the door to the café opened, and Professor Whatton came in, seemingly to buy takeaway coffee and cake. I felt foolishly taken aback that I hadn't known this was part of his weekly routine, but it was an added incentive—should I have been in need of one—for me to get back to work. As I joined him briefly at the counter to pay, Luigi said:-

'You must know each other from your laboratory, Professor. Dee has been telling me all about her work.'

His tone was capricious; and the Professor turned to me with what I perceived to be the same eyes of distrust that he might have turned on my errant colleagues. Anger welled in my breast:

'I've told you *nothing*, you useless man,' I said, and, with that, pushed over a display of glass jars containing oils and condiments from the counter that crashed messily at his feet.

I marched briskly from the café, leaving Luigi and the professor staring after me, as I recall, to the resounding echo of the cash-till.

*

Life at the laboratory returned to normal, or, at least, to a reasonably orderly way of working together for individuals who had new, irreversible knowledge of each other. My colleagues were neither here nor there, in my reckoning. One or two made a special effort to befriend me, but I was wary of accepting offers of drinks or society from characters who had proven themselves to be little better than the weak or dispossessed people who lived in the housing projects. And why now? What made me suddenly so worthy of their friendship?

The following spring brought my annual appraisal, and Professor Whatton wanted to know how I felt about working with him, or, more precisely, at his laboratory. Naturally, my response was that I thoroughly enjoyed it, and was keen to progress, and to take on whatever he felt me capable of. He marked me highly for all my work, including the accuracy of my research, my detailed cross-referencing, and my punctilious recording of results, but then he told me he had concerns about my team-fit, my 'ability to get on with my colleagues'.

'You will be required to work closely with these people, Dee, on some very important projects,' he said, eyeing me, not through his laboratory goggles, but his habitual horn-rimmed spectacles. 'It won't do to keep them at arm's length. Do you follow?'

'I'm not sure that I do,' I said, struggling to disguise my resentment. 'Would you have preferred it if I'd cavorted with them whilst on illegal and stolen drugs?'

'That's not what this is about,' he replied, irked that I had reminded him of the laboratory's unfortunate recent history. 'I want what's best for my team, and, actually, what's best for you, too. I know your sister Demmy, and I think we can find you something elsewhere altogether more suited to your skills and, um, personality.'

I awaited his dismissal, feeling utterly miserable, and wondering how much longer I would be expected to work with people who, for all I knew, might be laughing behind my back at Luigi's as we spoke.

'I will make some calls on your behalf,' said the professor, as I gathered myself to leave that day. 'And I will expect you to sign a confidentiality agreement before you go.'

'Sign a *what?*'

'It's standard procedure. To ensure non-disclosure of anything' (he paused at the word) 'that you have seen or been involved in during your time here.'

*

When Demmy spoke to me about a transfer to another laboratory, I noticed for the first time that she was no longer my high-handed sibling, loudly pointing out my relative failings, but a woman keen to make a sound decision that would both serve a member of her family as well as bolster her own professional worth. It was a win-win arrangement for her, my ingenious, ever perfectly positioned sister.

Initially, I wasn't excited at the prospect of tumour research, as the nearness of animals had freaked me out ever since I'd fallen off a pony at the age of eight, but I had a pleasant time at a welcome drinks party with the professors and their small team; and it became apparent that much of the animal work would be the domain of curator-types, not clinicians like myself. My colleagues were impressed that I had cut my teeth at Professor Whatton's laboratory, and no one seemed curious about why I had transferred. Once I knew that Demmy had been fully briefed about 'the incident', I did, however, allow myself to lose my temper about the unfairness of it. She poured me a large glass of red wine, and nodded along to my diatribe in the way she had grown accustomed to doing in order to placate me, before telling me what I should do next.

After a few weeks, she was confident enough that I had made a smooth transition into life at the animal lab to leave me to my own devices. My parents oversaw my acquisition of and removal to a new apartment, and, while I was working, had it decorated, and installed with my childhood piano, and other essential items from my previous home. I purchased some abstract art prints for my walls, painted with bold, geometrical patterns in colours that were sympathetic to my décor. I invited my colleague Tam for supper, as he was engaging and quite handsome, and I decided I would impress him with my repertoire of home-cooked meals: mussels in white wine and garlic; salmon wrapped in pastry; tenderloin of pork with mustard sauce. I was also keen for him to fuck me as it had been far too long since I had endured the fumbling hands and inane conversations of dull young men just to get relief from feeling their hard appendages inside me. Tam was surprised, and almost resistant to being invited into my bed so soon, but once he had the measure of what I offered, and had taken stock of the drawer of prophylactics and lubricants provided on his side of the bedroom, he became a willing accomplice. There was much to commend in having that itch scratched whilst adhering to the conventions of foreplay (that wider society seems to crave) such as sharing a refined dinner, or extending the occasional invitation to a family gathering. He seemed broadly impressed by my sisters, and vice versa. I didn't accept any return invites, however, and I neither knew nor cared if he had any family to speak of, which could well have been none, aside from what appeared to be a wretched cat with whom he was disproportionately obsessed. He eventually transformed himself from a reliably rough and ready bed-mate into someone who wanted to stay with me for the whole weekend, and find it necessary to compliment me on my physical appearance. To be honest, I would have been more content with a positive appraisal of my hunter's chicken. He began to buy me gifts: flowers, and a headscarf that he was bizarrely proud of, as it was made of silk, but all I could think of was, 'Why on earth would a woman born in this century wear a scarf over her head (or any which way)?' I remembered being bought a similar one by a previous limerent boyfriend who, I convinced myself, was comparing me unfavourably to my sister Demmy with her superior head of auburn hair, by intimating that mine might be better covered up. I decided to tell Tam we needed to re-evaluate things between us, and to stick to Friday night dinners followed by our original script of purely remedial sexual activity. He beat me to it, however, by confessing that he was intending to commit fully to being a vegetarian, and that he wanted more from a relationship than just providing an erection on demand. There was nothing else to say, as I had no intention of buying any new cookbooks, or resigning myself to a life of lettuce.

Having learned some resilience from my time negotiating the pitfalls of Luigi's, I soon adapted back to my former routine of supper for one— usually consisting of a delicious, uncompromising piece of meat or fish, and the demands-free company of my vibrator. Our paths still crossed at work, of course, which troubled him for longer than it did me. He had always displayed an irksome and inexplicable affection for the archivist girl whose name escapes me (Rita? Ruthie?), and I began to wonder whether she had more of his confidence the closer we got to ending things between us. So be it. Strange little brown girl with her soulful eyes and mannish hands. Perhaps she would be more willing than I was to listen to his tiresome cat stories, while she waited in a headscarf for him to get hard for her.

Professionally, I was able to make my mark in the laboratory, because I was by far the most skilled scientist. Whatton had taught me well, despite his disloyal discharge of my services. My clever sister had done right to place me there, but Demmy wasn't in the habit of making bad judgements. There was *one* aberration, of course, when she left her husband and her daughter for a spell to immerse herself in an affair with some dignitary in Geneva. We never got to meet him, this compelling man, but I imagine he was someone extraordinary. My parents drew a veil over this period in my sister's life because they were in denial that she could be anything less than perfect. However, this was my time to shine, as I managed to place her crestfallen fool of a husband in the temporary care of the archivist. *Rini!* That's her name! Before she took to mopping up the remains of my dalliance with Tam, she stepped into the breach in my sister's family, and played the caretaker wife and mother to young Lora. I don't think either of them suffered too many disadvantages as a result of my sister's absence, and, if anything, it gave them all a sense of what type of live-in curator they would need once Demmy was back, and expecting their second sprog.

Demmy continued to look out for me (in truth, she was probably forever in my debt!), as she made sure I was going to be out of harm's way when the pandemic hit; and she secured me the perfect job at the laboratory where they were working on the vaccine that would relegate *Virid20* to its proper place in history: a briefly rampant influenza bug. I imagined the look on Professor Whatton's face—and those of his feckless employees—when they got to read that I, Dee D'Abruzzo, was credited with a share in the research that finally got a vaccine into the arms of every citizen in the world! Yes, there would the cynics who would try to resist mass vaccination, but they would be treated in the same way any subversive element of society was treated: rounded up and vaccinated by force or, if they attempted to flee or to resist, they could expect to be captured, segregated, and put to work for the greater good of their own mutinous community.

For a while, I felt like Queen of the World—*king* would have been a lesser promotion. My sister's childhood shot at aspiring to achieve 'World Peace' seemed a poor second to my beating her at this one, soon to be universally ratified and celebrated achievement. I should have known, however, that she wouldn't rest on her demoted laurels for long, before she was reset on unseating my sense of sisterly superiority.

She asked to meet me at my flat, which was her preference, away from the eyes and ears of her husband and her offspring—the flat that had been set up for me after my rejection from Whatton's world: my haven of order and obedience. She said the vaccine was one thing, but *'Really Dee, in the greater scheme of things, people like us have higher callings to answer to, and more pressing problems to solve'*. The premature deterioration of the human brain, she insisted, was the greatest challenge that medical professionals faced in the modern world; and it was within our gift to make the difference between people dying too young with dementia as the major factor in their decline, or going on to live longer, more fulfilled lives. She ate my rabbit stew, and drank my vintage wine, and told me about confidential research she was overseeing that had involved injecting a synthetic protein (adapted from one naturally occurring in mammals) into the brains of mice that was having astonishing results. It seemed that around nine out of ten mice were dying, however one in ten was going on to show no signs of brain deterioration, physical decline, or, indeed, death.

'They generally fall asleep for around twenty-four hours then *slip away*— but there is one mouse they're calling *Genevieve*,' she enthused, pausing to blot her damp, red, dinner mouth on one of my freshly laundered napkins. 'The name being a take on the original woman from the bible story, who is now nearly eight years old. Eight years! Can you believe it? And she's still reproductive. I think she is now at the head of the most extraordinary family tree. There aren't enough 'greats' to usefully describe her anymore!'

I duly expressed my interest and incredulity.

'I don't need to tell you that the challenge we face is one of *ethics* when it comes to extending our research to the human population.'

Wasn't it ever thus? I'd said, although I added that I felt sure there would be people with dementia diagnoses who might be willing to take that leap of scientific faith like (misunderstood) lemmings, as they would have nothing to lose.

'Thereby hangs our other problem,' she went on. 'The change in the brain chemistry only seems to be effective (when it works) when we are testing it on young animals. There doesn't seem to be any appreciable benefit to administering it to older creatures.'

Then, I'd suggested, *we were unlikely to be able to continue with this particular line of research.*

'On the contrary,' said my sister. 'We just need a sample of young people who, shall we say, may easily "fall off the radar" without causing too much speculation, should they (unfortunately) not make it through the process. Old enough, obviously, to give consent. With guarantees, of course, that they would be afforded honourable memorials, which, for those from the dispossessed communities—curator types in the main— could be quite an incentive.' She gave a slight shrug at this point. 'If, indeed, they even *require* incentivising... Plus there is the potential for everlasting health and happiness! Did I mention that these mice are showing no signs of developing tumours, or any age-related conditions? We are on the brink of possibly the most important research known to medicine.'

For mice, I'd said.

'Which is where the challenge becomes so exciting! It's time we took the research to the next level. Only, not all of the medical councils are convinced we are ready. It goes without saying that I'm convinced by what I (and the team I've been involved with in Geneva) have seen to want to take that step. Can you imagine what this would mean for me, for us, for *the future of medicine* if we were able to deliver up a live result?'

I had made a bitter chocolate tart that I served in neat triangles decorated with mint leaves and raspberries. I watched her wince as the sharpness of the flavours briefly assaulted her taste buds, and derailed her from her speech. She licked her spoon and attempted to hang it on the end of her nose. I did the same, and we giggled like the children we once were— Demmy trying two or three times more to show she could balance her spoon for longer than I could.

'You could have a real role to play in this,' she went on, through the clatter of fallen cutlery. I gathered up the spoons and wiped down the table. I had been thinking of taking a trip up to the north, now that the pressing work at the laboratory was in abeyance. We had been slogging night and day, endless shifts (some of us) to ensure we kept up the rate of sample analysis and data verification. I had my mind, and possibly my heart, set on renting a cabin on a lake in the wilderness—every sane person's preference in the current climate of contagion—where I could sleep long hours, catch fish for my supper, make the acquaintance of a gamekeeper who would bring me fresh local kill, and maybe even become my holiday lover. I didn't really want the distraction of my sister telling me I still had more to do to prove myself.

A role for me? I'd said. *I don't see how.*

I had my back to her, and my front to the coffee machine. It was a sleek and sparkling gadget: the same make as Luigi's, only polished to a much more professional brilliance. I could see my face in it, and my sister's behind me, framed with her vibrant red hair giving the impression that part of my kitchen had caught fire.

'Our dear little friend Rini Sanchez,' she said, drumming her scarlet-tipped fingers on my marble counter. 'I don't have her confidence anymore—not that I ever really had it in the same way my beloved husband did! And, to be honest, appealing to her community would never be my forte. *You* on the other hand… this could be the making of you, now the heat is off your dabbling in a vaccine!'

What's your proposal, I'd said, or something similar. I imagined Demmy would have a plan, or was about to be the eloquent exponent of someone else's.

'She'll know people, youngsters. Doesn't she foster waifs and strays? She has a way with her. See what you can do to find a sample to take part in critical research. We believe we are at the stage of intravenous testing in young adults, and, if we can deliver up live results, we can embark on a sanctioned programme of tracking and longer-term analysis.'

My sister left after her coffee. Her mission had been accomplished. She hugged me tightly in the doorway, our bodies as close as they had been in our mother's womb. We no longer had the need to battle each other for a share of our mother's blood supply, or her breast milk. Now our instincts were honed to the challenge of jostling for supremacy *ex utero*.

I took a cheese platter to bed—each biscuit loaded carefully like a canapé to avoid crumbs or spillages—and opened my laptop. Dee had already sent me her council's proposal for the recruitment of candidates for the trial. It awaited human results to begin supporting its lofty remit. There was the assumption that some (maybe all) of the participants in the trial would not survive it, but that, after all, was what trials were for.

I followed the link to meet the snow-white super-mouse, Genevieve, and to see her preppy little face in close examination of the camera—her nose and whiskers aquiver, and her eyes as bright as polished apple pips. There were diagrams of the human brain with syringes penetrating the hippocampus; rows of phials of what purported to be a wonder-drug; and photographs of smiling couples looking at bright sunsets, as though they represented an alternative vision of a future where there were no age-related concerns or retirement communities. Lastly, there was a confidentiality agreement that I was invited to sign electronically as soon as I had read the document. I had barely licked the crumbs from my lips before Demmy had messaged my phone with a reminder to, '*Sign, Dee. Tonight.*'

It was as though Professor Whatton were back in my life, peering at me through his horn-rimmed spectacles, and treating me like a fool.

I closed down the window to Genevieve who had been trembling in the background, like she was making a plea for action, in some form, to be taken. For a few moments, I stared at my computer screen's saved landscape of a northern lake with a lone, grey-stone cabin on its shoreline, and I imagined solitude, and the feeling of bitingly cold air on my face, before falling swiftly asleep.

TORRAN

The trouble with me is I'm always bad news.

My mum said she had had the life sucked out of her and yet she still managed to get knocked up with me, *at her age,* after one stupid gamble. My dad was someone she owed a favour to, but she ended up paying for a broken window with what she called a lifetime of broken dreams. Now I'm older I understand exactly how she paid for her favour, but I think her dreams had been shattered long before I showed up.

I have a great-uncle and cousins who have always looked out for us, but I was raised to both hate them and expect them to make things better for us, because that was what my mum had taught me. She said there are those that have and those that have not, and we were in the second camp. I was always confused about how much we should do to try to make things better for ourselves, as I knew kids who played on the same streets as me who'd had the same bad luck, but their mothers somehow made things work, and were less angry. But there's nothing you can do when you're a kid—your hands are tied the same as if you've been roughed up and roped up in a daft game. You accept that's the way it is, and are just glad when there is food on the table, and your mum has had enough of what she needs to take the edge off, so as not to be clipping you round the head.

When she was good, she was great. It was me and her against the world, like we were two mates who didn't have to answer to a higher authority. My friends used to be in awe of her when she was in the mood for cooking and sharing her cans of beer, because they didn't have to suffer her when she wouldn't get out of bed for days, and when there was no breakfast on the table, or clean clothes to wear. I'd learned how to feed myself and mend the holes in my trousers before I knew how to count to twenty. All this was before the event that took us apart (in the normal way of things) forever. She did for us good and proper, my mum. Looking back, something was always going to happen, as she would wait until our lives were going OK, and then cause a rumpus. It was as if she just wasn't comfortable with peace, or comfort. Not when it came to mine, anyway. Rini was my foster mum from time to time, and she told me her mother used to do everything in her power to make her and her brother's and sister's lives happy and settled. I'm sure she wasn't telling me this to make me feel bad: just to explain how she felt about wanting to take care of me—like I'd been denied my birthright. I think she felt the same way about my grandad, who I otherwise thought of as an uncaring old bastard. Maybe he had been robbed of his birthright too.

When my mum was told I wasn't going to be living with her anymore, she made like she was having the heart torn out of her body, like someone was threatening to cut off her oxygen supply, or her access to daylight. It was hard to watch and not feel sorry for her, at least for people who hadn't spent their life knowing that she only had any feelings for them when her senses were under anaesthetic. Later, I came to terms with the fact that I had never had a mother who soberly tended to my fevers in the middle of the night, or held my head over a bowl of vomit until I felt better (instead of leaving me to wake up in my own mess). I had one who was neglectful, and shrieked like a wounded animal when her never-precious-until-that-moment son was going to be taken away from her to be offered a better life.

I had wanted a bicycle so badly I couldn't think straight or talk about anything else but getting one. I had friends with bikes in the commune who let me have turns, but it wasn't the same. They had earned them by doing jobs for their parents or running Governor errands. I knew, however, that no amount of work around the place, or chores for my mum, would earn me a bike. Even endless missions to bring her booze or score her drugs weren't enough, as this was no favour, just a means of keeping our disordered life from being pushed into chaos, with her cold and angry hands behind the shoving. It didn't stop me hassling her about it, though. I even tried telling her a bike would let me ride away, and she wouldn't have to worry about taking care of me anymore. The thought seemed to appeal to her for a bit—her eyes became little slits of interest through the smoke of her fag—but she dismissed it as a selfish plan of mine to get out of helping around the house like any decent kid should. I was so close to nicking one—there was a geezer who used to cycle to our allotment who parked his bike against the same bit of fence every week, and it would have been piss-easy. Then our relatives came by, as they often did, and offered to get one for me. I don't really know how best to describe them: a girl and a boy who were around my age whose grandfather was my grandmother's brother, so sort of cousins, I guess. They visited from time to time, sometimes with their parents, but mostly with just the grandad himself who was called Dillan. He was a bit of a pompous old cunt who seemed hell bent on taking charge of other people's lives, like he was on a mission. But when you don't have much going on in the way of help at home, you take what you're offered—at least that was my view, while my mum chose to think of him and the rest of her helpy family as 'interfering sods' who would do better to send us money. I'm not sure whether Dillan did actually send money too (my mother would never have admitted this to me in case I'd think thanks were owed); but he certainly arranged the cousins' visits from time to time, to try and make like things were normal. They were nice enough kids, even though we might have been speaking a different language sometimes, and they caught me out by pronouncing words in what they said was the 'right way' while I just said them how they looked like written down. No one took the piss, though, and, despite my mum's horrible behaviour to them, I quite liked them, and was glad of their company. My auntie would send them with packed lunches for us all that I would devour with no pretence at hanging back politely till others were ready to eat. I don't think they expected me to. My girl cousin Eliza used to put some grub aside for my mum—even though she had already shouted down she wouldn't go near their filthy food—because we all knew she would lose her uppity attitude once they had gone, and her hangover was making her ravenous. Like a cockroach scuttling out from its crack in the wall. I used to nick some of the left-overs myself, because I knew there might be nothing else to eat in our house for days after the cousins had been, plus I had to rely on food and water alone, while my mum always had booze and drugs to keep her going.

I'd told Eliza's brother Eric about my craving for a bike, and he knew exactly what I was on about. He was a good lad, Eric. A few years later I would be much more stuck on Eliza, when the nearness of her began to stir my prick. I'd wake up with that nagging need for someone to touch me, and to want to touch them back, and Eliza was the closest I'd got to that. But that was still years away—all I hankered after at this time was speed: a set of my own wheels, and the feeling of pedals under the worn-out soles of my shoes.

I'd been used to spending time away from my mum with other people—foster carers—who helped us out when she was more useless than usual. There was Rini; and another family, the Parkinsons, who would eventually become my regular parents and brothers. They all knew each other, and got along—Rini and the Parkinsons—so things were pretty sweet when it was decided that I should go to live with the family after the thing at home that fucked things over for good for my mum and me. My grandfather was on the scene by then—having pitched up from his hidey-hole in fuck knows where—and he made a bit of a fuss about me not getting to live with Rini instead. I swear to God the old git had the hots for her, but it just made sense that I got to live with a family. My grandfather drinks too much, and talks shit about how unfair life can be, which maybe explains where my mum got it from. It's all very well to rage against the world when you're off your box, and tooled up with the fantasy weapons of your addiction, but then to be a useless cunt when you're sober without the first idea how to help anyone except yourself.

Rini showed me what it was to *really* help someone. She never talked about what she was doing or why, but it seemed to me her life was shot through with acts of kindness, like the coloured ribbons of cloth that ran through the rug on my mum's bedroom floor—a thing of crazy beauty that had fascinated me from being a kid, before I noticed it was getting more and more spoiled with wine stains, and it was never picked clean of black hairs and threads of tobacco.

She had a friend with one arm and a fancy Governor's job in medicine who used to tell me Rini was her greatest inspiration, and I would do well to listen to her; and Rini would look at me and smile, shaking her head, as if these words couldn't possibly be true. She also knew a man called Joe who occasionally came to sit in her kitchen to talk about trees and plants, as if we'd never come across the bloody things ourselves before. He was a bit of a broken bugger, but he always left in a better mood, as though all he'd needed was for her to listen to him for an hour or two; and pour him some tea, and crack open a packet of biscuits. I met Tam, too, who I reckon was another bloke sweet on her. You get to notice these things when you become a man yourself and wonder how the hell you will ever get a chance with the opposite sex, apart from just talking rubbish to a girl in the hope she will talk back without taking the piss. Tam made it all about his cat, and Rini let him, even though it sounded like she was just a shitty old bag of bones and fur. *Mademoiselle* seemed to be all he had outside of their work at the laboratory, and, as no one would admit that, she became a sort of cat-cushion between the two of them, that absorbed all their unspoken feelings. It was kind of weird, but kind of alright at the same time.

But I should get back to the story of my bicycle, as it changed the course of my life. Eric must have told his grandfather about my desire for a bike, because they decided it was something that every kid had a right to own, and not something I should be borrowing from other kids. (I didn't tell Eric about my plan to nick old Derek's bike, as this might have changed their minds). Dillan wouldn't have had a clue about what sort of a bike to get for me, but Eric did. I imagine it was just like one he would have owned himself, and it hardly bothered me (as it would have bothered my mum) that Eric and Eliza had probably owned half a dozen bikes already.

When it arrived, it was the best fucking thing I had ever seen, and I almost wanted to devour it like I used to devour my auntie's picnics; but Rini had been teaching me about the importance of showing gratitude, no matter how desperate my need might feel. I thanked everyone in turn, Eric and Eliza; my uncle and aunt; and my great-uncle Dillan who I nearly knocked over with a hug—a strange and clumsy moment for both of us—because I knew he was the one who would have paid for it, and made it happen.

I went out on my bike that day, and didn't come back for hours. I think I missed them all leaving our house and heading back to their own homes, but I didn't care. I'd done enough thanking, and needed to get down to the business of riding the fucker.

Whenever I left home and went out in search of adventures (even before I had my freedom wheels), I never completely forgot about my mum. I expect she forgot about me for hours on end, until she needed something, or a mate knocked for me and reminded her she had a son. I was glad to break free from her and our dismal little building in the commune for a bit, but I never wished her any harm, or wanted to get back to find her not there—whatever wasted state I might find her in.

On the day my new bike arrived, she had chosen not to come down until our relatives had left, and when she had, she tore the place to bits, smashing crockery and breaking up a lot of the furniture. My memory plays an image from that day of me looking down on the scene from above: I'm on my knees, trying to figure out how to screw the legs back onto a kitchen chair, so she can sit down and stop the blood from running down her arms. All the while, I'm calm, because I know my bike is in the passage, out of harm's way, and it's waiting to take me away again as soon as it can.

I don't know how we made it to bed that night, but we did, only to be woken again in the early hours in the glare of bright lights and raging heat, our ears filled with the wailing of sirens. I remembered trying to fight off a fireman to get to where I thought I'd find my bike, but his body was a solid pillar of resistance, believing he was battling to save my life, and not knowing that holding me back was threatening to break it into pieces. I screamed for my bicycle like another kid would have screamed for his mum. I guess I already knew how the fire had started and why. I think this was the first time I realised I actually hated her.

Rini has talked to me about compassion. Easy for her, she said, when her life had been filled with happiness and love. Even I, Torran, who had come from nothing, could see that Rini's life had been far from perfect; but she just seemed to know how to put a brighter spin on things. She taught me that I didn't hate my mum, just that I hated not feeling loved by her. After my first bike, I think I learned to prize my friendship with Rini more than anything else. She was just there when I needed her, colouring in the blanks and never wanting no thanks. Bikes came and went once I'd moved out of the commune, and my mum had gone to live in a safer place with the nut jobs. Even my grandfather Art got me one: a shitty second-hand one, but a bike is a bike. He said a bike was only as good as its rider, and he wasn't wrong, the old scrote. I rode the crap out of it, and never worried about someone nicking it because it didn't look like it was worth the effort. But, in truth, it was my best bike ever, because I never felt beholden to Art for giving it to me, and when I sped around on it, slamming it between my legs and kicking at the pedals, it felt like I was fighting my family for shitting on me, and this was them taking their punishment like they knew they should: Art, my mum, all of them. There's a lot to be said for giving a boy a bike.

Mr and Mrs Parkinson—Roy and Jean—encouraged me to call them Mum and Dad, which, after a while, I did, just as naturally as my foster brothers James and Mark. It felt weird at first, like when my mum used to ask me (in front of other people) to pucker up and give her a kiss, and I felt I had no choice, even though it curdled my insides to do so. My brothers could have taken the piss out of me (like Eric and Eliza could have) as I was a bit of a weedy git compared to both of them, but they never did. We had the odd skirmish when one of us went down too hard on a football, or wanted to spend so long in the shower for a wank that we were going to run out of hot water; but mostly we got along just great. My new parents were kind and responsible—a bit like my great-uncle Dillan, although a fair bit younger and not quite so up themselves. I don't know if they ever met my mum—I expect they did—and I always wondered if she found them easier to like because they weren't the blood relatives that she despised so much, and you never saw any hint of disappointment, judgement, or pity behind my adopted dad's speccy-eyes. When I say 'like', I don't think my mum ever really liked anyone, but she may have been OK about the Parkinsons because they took me off her hands without suggesting that any of it was her fault. Perhaps this is what finally gave her leave to push a needle once too often into her veins, and mistakenly (or not) take her own life, as she knew she didn't have to worry about me anymore, and, maybe more importantly, wouldn't die thinking I would end up with her 'interfering sod' of an uncle Dillan.

He was beside himself when the news reached him—I heard it described as 'disproportionately so'—but I think his grief was more about his failure to make things right than the loss of his niece. My grandfather explained to me, a bit sheepish-like, that Dillan had given a lot of himself trying to do right by my grandmother and my mum; and I should respect his commitment to his family, despite his pomposity. Not that I didn't, in my own way, but I still felt pissed off that this talk of commitment hadn't made any difference to *him,* as my mum was his own daughter. Yeah, Art?

I didn't want to go to my mum's funeral, but Rini convinced me I should in case I looked back in years to come and regretted it. A few years have gone by, and I don't believe she was right; but, at the time, I didn't want to seem even more weird to my new family and friends than I was already, so I involved myself. My grandfather sat at the back of the church in his smelly old coat, with Rini at his side, and I sat with Eric and Eliza. Someone I didn't know made a speech, but I reckon it was written by Dillan. It was about weeds and flowers, and reminded me of Rini's friend Joe, and how people use random things to describe their feelings rather than just telling it like it is. But then, if I'd told Eliza I wanted to take her clothes off and fuck her in the churchyard rather than saying, 'Hello, how nice to see you, how are you and your boyfriend Kyle?' the day would have gone a whole lot worse than it did. Mark and I made enough of a mess of things by necking a bottle of vodka at the party afterwards (Rini kept telling me it was a 'wake' not a party, but, to us Parkinson lads, it was just another excuse to rip things up a bit, and get sneakily pissed).

It wasn't a horrible day for me, my mother's funeral. I'd known worse. There was the hassle of a dressing down from my adopted mum and dad when we got home from the wake-party, but no one was about to ground me on such a difficult day for a young lad, so Mark and I hopped out to get some more beers, and meet up with a couple of girls. The girl called Jade made my fucking year by tossing me off in the bushes, and waiting around until I was up for it again, and letting me shoot off into her knickers. Goodbye and thanks for nothing, Mum. There are much nicer women in the world than you ever were, even after a skinful of booze or a noseful of powder. There are women like Jade.

Life took a bit of a dive when the pandemic hit. My parents were pretty laid back when stories first came on the news, and they didn't care much for gossip, so their initial take on the virus was that it was likely to blow over if we all just took sensible precautions, and got on with our lives. They meant stuff like throwing away used tissues (never a challenge in a houseful of randy but easily rumbled boys), washing our hands more carefully, and stocking up on cold cures. Then it became clear we were going to have to do much more than that.

One day, Mark was chasing me home through our back alley, and I had gotten so fast lately he had had to stop and lob one of his shoes at me to slow me down. I was shouting back at him that if he wasn't such a fat wanker he'd stand a better chance, then suddenly our mum was standing in our way with a face like thunder. We thought we were proper for it, but she just said, 'Boys, this is serious. You won't be going back to school tomorrow. We're in what the Council is calling *lockdown*.' The first part of what she was saying was so great that we didn't really process the misery of what the second part would bring.

We had a computer that lived in the kitchen, and we used to take turns with it for our schoolwork. Dad decided this would now belong to James who was studying for important exams, and he brought another one home from his place of work for me and Mark to share. The Decision had been made years before that I was destined for a role as a Curator (surprising no one, least of all me), whereas Mark was a smart kid—like the rest of his family—and was bound for something brilliant, no doubt, in engineering or medicine. But it was a cool move that I was given an equal share in the use of the device, even though I wished I'd been overlooked once *virtual* classes began, and I had to listen to teachers droning on at me for hours while I was stuck at home. I had gotten to thinking lately that I might like to do something like what Rini did at her laboratory, because she got to use dangerous chemicals and deal with life and death stuff— and I've always had a soft spot for animals. The filing would be a bit of a bore, but Rini says it would concentrate my mind which does have a tendency to need reining in from time to time. Plus I would be working with Tam, who is an alright bloke. I'd met another Governor there—a bird called Dee—although she wasn't so matey when I first met her, probably because she thought I was too far beneath her concerns to care. Rini said I wasn't to take it to heart: that she was a dead clever woman, and probably had her head too full of critical stuff to be chatty. Not then, anyway, *ha!* She buggered off to work somewhere else, in the end, and good riddance. It wasn't the last I saw of her, though.

Anyways, I knew I had to keep my grades up or I wouldn't get the chance to apply to the laboratory. There would be plenty of kids like me scratching at that door, knowing if they didn't shape up they would only be able to clean the windows or sweep the floors in the place, which would absolutely suck. Rini says there's a dignified place in the world for every Curator, but I would sooner ride off the edge of a cliff than find myself at the arse end of things. She says I'm like my grandfather; and I need to turn my words into actions, which makes me think I'm still a good apple in a bag of crap ones, but if I don't look sharp I'll catch the same rot as him and my mother. I think of that whenever I'm having a tough time toeing the line.

The truth is lockdown tested us much more than we could have realised when we were first told about the restrictions—the clever kids too, not just the dumb-ass ones like me. It's like we lost the will to do anything except loll around. We could still go out on our bikes, but not too far; and Dad eventually drew up an exercise plan for me and Mark to get us out of the house as much as possible. It was OK, but it got boring after a couple of weeks, as it was just him and me, and we weren't able to meet up with any of our mates. Mum had a tough time of it as her mum (who was sort of my grandmother—a living one who hadn't been a mess like the one I never knew who was married to Art) was in a care facility, and she wasn't allowed any visitors. Eventually Mum was able to go and see her through her window, but it was way up on the second floor, and the old lady was getting more and more confused about why she was on her own. The worst thing was when she caught *Virid20* and died in the hospital without anyone she knew with her. I imagined if I was dying it wouldn't much matter who was there or not, especially if I was old and a bit mad; but my mum took it hard. It meant she was really out of sorts for weeks, and Dad had to take on most of the jobs and decisions around the house. I was glad he was so strong at this time because her loss of spirits was reminding me of my real mum, and all the bad things that happen when you slip under the waterline. It seemed to knock the stuffing out of her. She was always really good at planning meals and family events, but she seemed to stop caring, and was wearing the same clothes day after day; and her hair—that was always cut into a neat shape like a bike helmet—grew too long with a great grey stripe down the middle, because no one was allowed to go to the hairdressers. She just lost herself for a bit.

We had a glimmer of hope that normality might be returning—or at least we were expected to go back into school for a while—but as winter started to kick in, people were getting sick again, and we had to return to our previous level of imprisonment. At this point, Mum had been able to have her hair done, and was getting back to her old self. She started to bake bread, and even showed us lads how to make cheese. We weren't in such bad spirits as we'd seen our mates—and even had a bit of action with the girls. We told ourselves that this wouldn't be forever, and our patience would pay off when a vaccine was available, which we understood the scientists were working round the clock on making and testing, so they could 'get it into our arms' as soon as possible. I said I would happily be a guinea pig if it meant getting things back to normal, but my mum said I shouldn't say such things as we had no idea what would be in a vaccine that had only taken a few months to perfect, when they normally take years—and she would think twice before having it, or encouraging her sons to, when the time came. This made my dad cross—which wasn't like him at all—and he said her attitude was 'appalling' given the year we'd been having; and my parents had the first full-blown row that I had ever seen them have. It was like one crap thing after another, starting with the death of our grandmother, because then my dad—or Roy, as I began to think of him as again—dropped a massive bollock by telling us boys that he was going to be leaving our mum as he had 'begun a relationship' with one of his colleagues at work. More than just the shitshow of this piece of news, we had to work through the likelihood (which soon became the certainty) that he had been meeting her for sucks and fucks while the rest of us were living like prisoners! No wonder he had been so quick to do the supermarket runs while Mum was bedbound with grief! It made me sick to my stomach. I talked to Rini as best as I could on my mobile phone, but some conversations just aren't best had like that. She wanted me to know (like I needed telling) that none of this was my fault, and I couldn't have prevented it happening. That was kind of obvious, but I still felt shite about maybe being that bad apple that had gotten into someone else's bag and brought a maggot with it. Then I decided I didn't want to talk to nobody for a bit, least of all on a phone.

James kind of took on the role of the dad in the house, which Rini said he might; and this was OK until it started to feel like he was pushing us about, and being much stricter than Roy had ever been. Rini said to follow his advice, and to be grateful for his guidance, and I said, 'Yeah, whatever', but wanted to be looking out for myself.

There's always been a bit of anger in me—a firework in my belly that just needs a spark to set it off—but I imagined it was down to my useless mother. It seemed there was something similar waiting to blow in Mark's belly, too—unless of course he had just caught the rot from me, 'cos his mum was a pretty decent woman. I felt bad about upsetting her now she was left in her armchair most nights with the grey stripe back in her hair, watching other people's made-up life stories on the TV while her husband was off writing a whole new dirty book without her. But my skin was itching and burning if I sat still, and I was desperate to be out looking for action. Jade was now always part of my night-time plans as she was on the scene, and it would be her and me at it in the bushes or the bus shelter come the end of the evening, when Mark was off scoring drugs or hitting on some other girl. I got to thinking of her as my girlfriend, and started worrying about who else she might let up inside her if I couldn't make it out and about. Stupidly I asked her if I was her bloke, and she made fun of me, and asked if I was jealous. I said of course not, but she hurt my pride and ignited that firework, and I made good and sure I pumped my load into her deep and hard that night. I left her on the ground, and was worried I might have hurt her, but she rolled over and lit herself a fag. I wanted to hang around and talk about it all, but Mark was calling me away, wired as an electrified cat. I said, 'See you around', and she said the same back, but mine was a question, and hers wasn't.

We nicked a car that night. Fucking stupid prank, but it was a total gas at the time. I hadn't the first idea how to drive, which is why, when it was my turn, I totalled it into a tree. Mark had had some lessons with Roy and was OK behind the wheel; and he turned his face to mine—crazy white, it was, against the blackness in the car—like he was the sensible kid, and I was the troublemaker. I opened the car door and ran. I went back to where I'd left Jade earlier that evening, but she was gone. When I got home there was a police car waiting and I was in deep shit. The policeman was a smug cunt who was too fat for his uniform, so he looked like he was bursting out of it at the neck like a sausage you'd cooked too hot and too fast. He reminded me of my grandfather Dillan, and my first thought was thank fuck *he* was now too old to be getting up in my business. My second thought was what Rini might think, and I felt like a twat. Then the policeman said I should have treated my foster parents with more respect, so I told him to cock off.

Mark didn't get away without James skinning his lardy arse, but I knew, as a Governor in the making, he would soon be able to wipe his slate clean with the authorities. His pedigree was a lot better than mine when it came down to it, and, like I said at the beginning, I'm always bad news. Eventually, Rini worked out whose car we'd nicked and made me write them a letter of apology, but there was a way to go before I got to that point in my story.

Just when restrictions were starting to ease for a second time, and spring was in the air, I was shackled to an ankle cuff that meant I couldn't get very far without it sounding an alarm. Obviously I was keen to push my luck, and wait to see which gormless knob from the Council would have to come out to switch it off, and turn me around. I got to know some of them quite well, and gave them all suitable names ranging from Cunty to Skullface, depending on who showed up. Eventually of course, I worked out what my 'range' was, and served the rest of my time without bothering the useless arseholes.

As luck would have it, my range included getting as far as the communes where I used to live, and where most of the not-rights and misfits could be found. This was either an epic piece of dickheadedness by the Council or part of a bigger plan to drive people like me deeper into the ditch where they thought we belonged. It was a great place to lose my mind a little from time to time, but I saw too many of my mother's (and probably my grandmother's) faces in the alleys and the doorways to lose it completely. I avoided the area where I had grown up because it felt too much like an invitation for history to repeat itself. I thought I saw Jade from time to time, but I was probably mistaken; and it hurt like a knee in my bollocks that she hadn't looked out for me once curfews were over. Maybe she had heard about my ankle tag and didn't want to be infected with the same rot—and who could blame her. She wasn't a daft girl, and I imagined she would be working in the coffee house again and getting back to her training to be a hairdresser. I had some weird moments when the thought of her touching men's hair made me want to punch walls; but I told myself to get over it, man, and that she was more likely to be touching women's. But I missed her. Not just the warmth of her skin and the comfort of her insides, but the fact we shared stuff rather than keeping it to ourselves. And for brief moments, despite her careless words, it was all about me.

I suppose my loneliness, and the awkward feelings now between me and Mark, was why I started to go to a drinking house on the edge of the commune where I was born. I was too young to buy booze anywhere else, but this was one of those places where nobody asked any questions as long as you had some cash. My mum still gave me an allowance, and I was able to run a few errands again, so I had enough for a reasonable session from time to time.

I had learned from Rini that there is good and bad in everyone, and I became quite a people watcher, sat listening to all sorts of drunken shit at the bar while earning free drinks for my trouble.

One night, I'd clocked a stranger sat on her own by the window, making a meal of one glass of wine, and folding a paper coaster into what looked like an impossible number of squares. When she was done, she undid it and started over; all the while looking around at the people who came and went. A proper fish out of water. She was nothing like the other women who drank in there—most of them were red-faced and toothless, and in ratty old clothes—as she was wearing a short office-type skirt with black tights and flat shoes, with one of her long legs wrapped around the back of the other like a snake climbing up a tree. Her legs were slim and sexy, and the thought of getting between them made me itch a little. But she was too old for me, and uptight, with a fierceness about her that took the fire out of the fantasy.

To my surprise—after I'd been concentrating on a guy feeding his pet rat on a string with pieces of broken bread and cheese—the woman got up from her table and came over, making like she knew me and I knew her. As the light from the bulb above the bar brought her face to life, I realised she was one of the Governors from Rini's lab! It was stuck-up Dee, out of place in a shitty drinking house on the wrong side of town. She removed her face mask and smiled in a way that made me wonder if I'd imagined she'd once looked at me like I was a turd she might cross the street to avoid stepping in. She used my name; she bought me a drink. She bought me another drink, all the while talking some bollocks about her work at her new lab, occasionally touching her nose and glancing down at my ankle cuff, as if she was taking it in, but not thinking I'd noticed. I noticed alright—in fact, I crossed my leg, so it was right there between us to embarrass her, like I was an old git who'd been for a slash and left his pecker out. But she still didn't mention it.

I offered to buy her a drink, but she said no, like I might have been planning on poisoning her, so I said, 'What's the matter, do you think I'm trying to poison you?' and she laughed at that which gave me a bit of a kick, given she had gone out of her way to get in my company. It felt kind of weird, given there could be nothing else she could want from me, apart from my company; and even weirder as she was old enough to be, well, not my mother, exactly, but certainly my teacher or someone.

She asked me if I'd eaten, so I said no, even though I'd had dinner at home before I came out, because I never say no to food. It comes from a time when I didn't know if my last meal actually might be my last—or at least the last one in a fucking long time. She said would I like to have dinner at her flat? It was my turn to laugh, and I drew full attention to my ankle iron by sticking my foot out. I said, 'Yes, if you only live round the corner!' and this was when it got really strange, 'cos she waved her hand and said, 'Oh, don't worry about that, I just have to make a call.'

She walked away from the bar and put her phone to her ear, and in what seemed like no time at all, a goon in black clothes had appeared at the door (not so visible that he would spook the drinkers inside), and only went and unlocked my cuff. He spoke to me like I had been the one making the plea to be let loose while she stood aside with her arms folded, taking it in and confirming she would have it back on me in a few hours. He was gone, leaving me staring at her holding my fucking ankle iron like some kind of prize she'd won for me at the fair. It was one of the craziest moments of my life.

She drove us to her flat in a car that smelled of the cleaner my mum used if we spilled stuff on the sofa—a speedy journey with quick and clever jerks of the wheel like she was up against the clock. I guess I'd had enough of what I needed that night not to worry one bit about what the rest of it might bring—and maybe even to invite it to bring on something else, something new and exciting.

I sat in her shiny kitchen where she poured me wine—thick, purple, juicy stuff that tasted like a more expensive bottle than my grandfather would be able to afford. I made a note that I would tell him—boasting, like—about what I'd been drinking next time I saw him. She slipped off her shoes and, in her stockinged feet, hopped around her cooker stir-frying vegetables and bits of seafood that I could smell but didn't know exactly what they were. When the meal appeared before us in two bowls of noodles, I ate several mouthfuls before I had to stop and say, 'What is this all about? Why have you brought me here, and what do you want?'

She was taken aback, and put down her cutlery with a serious change to her looks. She said, 'Torran, it's more about what *you* want,' and she eyeballed me like she was possessed. It freaked me out a bit, but I wasn't one for running scared.

'I guess I'll need a ride home at some point,' I said, plain as you like.

She stopped eating and pushed her plate away like my real mum used to when she was going to give me a hard time, as though food wasn't a basic need of hers, and I had a nerve to suggest it was one of mine. Jeez, the number of times I had gone back to that abandoned plate and scraped it clean with my own spoon.

'I want to offer you a way out,' she said.

'A way out of what?' I replied.

'Out of your wasted life,' she said, sharply. Her mouth twitched in judgement of me and people like me.

'What do you mean?' I asked her. 'You can't make me born again, to parents who give a fuck.'

My own words took me a little by surprise, and maybe her too, as she drew her meal back and carefully forked some more of it into her mouth: fat prawns that she'd speared like they were the easiest prey on her plate.

'No, I can't do that,' she said. 'But I can be useful to you.'

'Like how?'

'Tell me what you want, and you can have it. I imagine I must have *something* you want.' She took a swig of her wine and pressed her reddened tongue between her lips.

I thought fuck, she's coming on to me, which made my heart pound in my throat, but scared the shit out of me at the same time. This was a woman who had worked with Rini and was someone she respected. She was a Governor, for fuck's sake.

'Not really,' I said. 'I have a girlfriend.'

I felt like a bit of a dick, but she didn't react, as though she was neither disappointed nor relieved by what I'd said.

'It doesn't have to get in the way of your girlfriend. Does she have a name?'

'Jade,' I said, through a nervous cough, and prayed I sounded like I wasn't lying.

'Does she give you everything you want?'

'She doesn't *pay* me!' I said and laughed at the conversation we were having and the prickishness of my situation.

'Well, there it is,' she said, and sat up smartly in her chair. '*Money*! I can pay you, Torran. If you do something for me in return.'

Her house was fancy, her food and wine were high class. If she wasn't trying to get into my pants, I figured there might be something good about to go down in this strange relationship. I guess I reverted to type and took the bait a little too soon.

'You name it,' I said. 'What do you want me to do?'

'Well, you must have heard that I was chosen to work on the vaccine?'

'I think I might have heard something…'

She flinched as though it were crazy to think this wasn't everyone's hot topic. Jeez, the virus was getting to be old news…

'Despite what most people think, it's a relatively straightforward remit. More than anything we now just need people to volunteer themselves for drugs trials.'

'Yeah, I guess. Like guinea pigs.'

'A little further up the food chain than that,' she said, with a smirk. Smug bitch. So she had been cruising the shitholes of the communes looking for lab rats, and tonight it was my turn. 'People like you can make all the difference between success and failure, life and death, in all sorts of areas of research.'

'It doesn't exactly sound above board,' I said, thinking this would be what my mum—my foster mum—would have said. I was beginning to regret leaving her at home again, possibly worrying about what I was up to. It seemed ridiculous to ask to have my ankle tag put back and for a ride home; but it's what I did.

A week later, however, I'd had time to think. More people were dying from *Virid20* and life was looking like a rollercoaster of opportunities and disappointments. My mum Jean was refusing to leave the house: sending moody James out for everything. Mark had seen Jade and she was out of work and using. I felt like my head was boiling with the need to do something epic. I messaged Rini and made out that I needed Tam's or Dee's numbers, to ask about jobs, which wasn't a complete lie. Rini didn't question me: she even said Dee had been asking after me (result!) and coughed up.

Dee called me back straight away, and said she would pick me up from the drinking house. She said I wouldn't regret it, and my ankle tag would be off permanently sooner rather than later. I said I needed some money up front—a lot of money—and she agreed. I dropped a bag off at Jade's who took it from me, standing dumb as a statue on her mum's doorstep. Dumb and pregnant with someone's baby, and I was hoping to fuck it was mine, because I had come to realise that I loved her and needed her more than anything I'd ever known.

Rini (II)

The sun rose on a day of twin disasters for a woman called Rini Sanchez.

A man had been found hanged in his apartment, and hers was the last number the police had found on his phone. He was a local gardener who kept himself to himself. He was, also, the man who had inadvertently driven his lorry into the path of an oncoming vehicle several years earlier, killing both of the occupants. These unfortunate people had been Rini's parents.

It was a Saturday morning, and Rini wasn't expected at work that day. She went straight to the police headquarters where she was asked to help identify the dead man from his phone and a handful of photographs. She wasn't permitted to see the body of Joe Solomon, as they decided the sight of his blue and bloated head would be overwhelming. She explained that she worked with deformity and death every day, and felt that someone should do him the honour of bidding him farewell; but her request was refused. She was told his door had been daubed with the word 'Murderer'—not for the first time, apparently, but he had been rigorous in painting it out (and careful never to mention it to Rini whenever they met) until it had reappeared for a final, fateful time when he no longer had the will to find his paintbrush.

Satisfied that Rini could be of no further help, she was allowed to leave the building, and she headed first to her sister's, then to her brother's, house. Becks was in her dressing gown, bleary-eyed, and suitably taken aback by the news. She offered her sister coffee, and a chance to reminisce a little about their beloved parents whom she still missed dreadfully; but Rini refused, as she wanted to make haste to Reggie's house before a visit would get in the way of his family's weekend plans.

Reggie and his wife insisted she had breakfast with them while their children were still asleep. Maya was a sweet person who reacted with shock and dismay—any form of bad news would cause her brow to pucker, and make her seem a little exhausted by it, regardless of whether or not it impacted on her. She looked anxiously into both Rini's and Reggie's faces as she poured their coffee.

The decision never to tell her siblings that she had befriended Joe after her parents' accident was one she stood by now he had joined them in death. They would not have understood her moral obligation, and she remained certain it would have confused and even angered them.

97

When Maya left the kitchen to attend to her stirring babies, Rini told her brother that Joe had been regularly harassed by thugs who seemed hell bent on vengeance. These days, Reggie had flecks of white in his morning stubble, and they gleamed like shards of sea salt as he rubbed his chin in contemplation of her news. Sat at his table, the pensive big brother she remembered from her youth—weighing his words carefully before he spoke, only mildly distracted by the sound of his household waking noisily upstairs—Rini felt a familiar ache of love for someone she felt bound to for life, come what may.

'I can only say he won't be missed much,' he said. 'Hadn't his wife already left him?'

'I believe so,' said Rini. 'But he was trying to make a decent life for himself.'

Their conversation was obliged to turn to lighter matters as the children arrived, clamouring for attention, all of them wanting to sit on their auntie's knee, and to demand her help in choosing their breakfast cereal.

When Reggie showed his sister to the door, however, he returned to the reason for her visit.

'I don't know of anyone who would have remembered Joe Solomon, or what he did.' he said. Reggie still headed up the council that presided over the affairs of the dispossessed. 'And certainly no one who would be persuaded to paint abusive messages on his front door.'

Rini left her brother's house, sadly convinced that a person could be persuaded to do anything if they were desperate enough, and if their reward was suitably satisfying. She rested her head against the window of the bus on her ride home, mindful—and sorrowful—that she had said nothing to Reggie about the word 'Murderer' that had repeatedly defaced Joe's door, and that had driven him to take his own life. Her brother had been deceiving her, as she had been deceiving him; only the foundation of their respective acts of deceit could not have been more different.

Joe was gone, and she wanted to believe that he would now be able to rest in peace. There was nothing more for her to do, except to continue to tend the various plants that he had introduced in good faith into her balcony garden—ferns, with their innocuous spear-like leaves, and

98

cyclamen, with their hanging but hopeful (and frost-defiant) pink faces—and never to forget a man who deserved to be remembered for more than just two days' horror when he had accidentally caused the death of a pair of strangers, and deliberately brought about his own.

More bad news had been lying dormant on her phone while she had been fretting over poor Joe. There were several missed calls from Jean Parkinson who was the adopted mother of her young friend Torran. Months of restrictions while they had battled *Virid20* were starting to wear people down, and it was generally agreed that small groups of people should be allowed to gather once again, so Rini invited Jean to come round to her flat. Jean arrived looking careworn, wringing her hands together with fingers that still found the wedding ring to twist for comfort and reassurance despite no longer having the husband who had put it there.

Torran is gone, she said. He had been missing for two nights, and Jean was beside herself. She had resisted going to the police as her son had been in trouble with them lately, and she was afraid of making things worse for him; but she was starting to feel desperate. Had Rini heard anything from him? Rini checked her phone again, and had to confirm he hadn't been in contact for a couple of weeks. On any other day, she would have urged Jean to ask the police for help, as she knew that the sooner a hunt for a missing person could be initiated the more successful the outcome was likely to be; but she couldn't dismiss from her mind how coldly and ineffectually they had dealt with Joe's affairs that morning. Furthermore, she couldn't shake the thought that even her own brother, despite being her own flesh and blood, was another example of a Governor who was inclined to take more than the law into his own hands.

If Torran had run away, he would be running scared, and he would need to be persuaded to see sense by someone he trusted.

ARTHUR (III)

Arthur Smith took some time to rise and shine that morning, as he had succumbed to the charming, but ultimately anaesthetic, company of a bottle of single malt whisky the night before. He woke with what felt like a head stuffed with cotton wool soaked in alcohol, and the fumes were making their peat-infused escape down his nostrils. On balance, however, he had known worse starts to his day.

The postman brought the mail, and a small dog called Bryony delivered it to his lap. He was looking after the creature while its owner was in hospital having her hip replaced (or, rather, had been, and was now in respite care somewhere to fully recover) and, as she was a neighbour of his friend Steve—and Steve was always keen to give Arthur a canine-based project now they no longer pursued birds of prey—it fell to him to do the honours. Arthur would never have volunteered, as this wasn't in his nature. The last time he had countenanced volunteering, he had still been the proprietor of the ironmonger's, and a pair of scouts—one was a girl-scout with fetching plaits and a necktie—had come in asking for donations for a raffle. He referred them to Noley, and she ended up volunteering to run one of the stalls at their fair. That was Noley—always stepping into the breach when the breach could easily have been circumnavigated by offering up a few plant pots and a watering can, instead of a whole afternoon in the company of snot-nosed scouts.

Taking on the temporary care of Bryony, however, was no hardship in comparison, and he soon had the little dog trained to fetch his mail, and his shoes, one by one, and—for his own idiotic amusement—to answer to the name of Brian. He liked to see her little black-and-white head tilted in enquiry at the mention of her almost-name, knowing she was programmed to do the bidding of this foolish old man, because he was the keeper of the kibble, and the provider of freshly killed rabbit (which, he suspected, her owner would not have approved of for her dinner bowl). Fortunately for his young canine charge, Steve 'knew a man with a gun'. This, Arthur decided, would remain their secret, along with her nickname.

That morning, Bryony brought him news that anchored him to his armchair for longer than he would have anticipated, allowing the kettle to whistle itself hoarse before he put it out of its misery by making a jug of coffee.

'Well, well, well,' he said repeatedly to himself, and to Bryony, who hadn't enjoyed the kitchen commotion, but was now back in her basket, resting with her nose safely tucked into her belly.

It seemed Noley was getting married; taking herself a husband; tying the knot: a range of expressions sprang to his mind like euphemisms (if euphemisms were necessary) for the state of union between a man (this one was called Edward to begin with, then became Ed as the letter affectionately unfolded) and a woman who, to put it bluntly, had once been Arthur's common-law wife. She was the one who had stayed around the longest: who hadn't allowed his boredom of her to put her off or put her out. She took on his elderly parents when he would have sooner relinquished them into the haphazard care of social services. She used to pour his wine, and sip her own soft drinks (which he occasionally swapped for something with bubbles that instantly turned her cheeks pink, and made her lips go numb), and listen tirelessly to his tirades against the world, pausing only to remove his trousers to indicate she'd heard enough for one day, and intended to send him to sleep with the sucker punch of sex. Noley left him, eventually (with no discernible hard feelings) to take care of another relative—this time a blood relative, so more obviously deserving of her benevolence—and, seemingly. somewhere along the way, had met and was about to marry another man. She was no spring chicken, Arthur marked, as he re-read her letter, despite being a dozen years or so his junior; but she clearly had always had marriage on her mind. She had once been inquisitive about Arthur's history on that front, but he could be a cantankerous sod, so she had chosen to settle for his summary of that side of his life before they had begun their own relationship, forged (where else?) in the local pub, as, 'There was never anyone memorable, and one or two I'd rather leave unmentionable'. Looking back, it was a brutal way to encompass, amongst all his other dalliances, his short marriage to Amber from another world, and his accidental creation of a child, but, once Noley's early curiosity had been extinguished, neither of them had the confidence (on her part) or the courage (on his) to raise it again.

Arthur had never wanted marriage. He had been bullied into it by an overbearing older brother who had discovered his sister was up the duff. His own parents' marriage was the example he had no intention of emulating—two people obliged to keep residing under the same roof despite having nothing in common apart from joint custody of a pointless piece of paper and a small, confused boy. He wanted a woman, of course—in fact, he wanted as many women as possible—although, as he faced the end of things, he realised he had longed more for the attention of a mother than for the comfort of a lover, and he came to concede that the absence in his childhood of the former had cursed him with a lifelong obsession with the latter.

He was happy for Noley, however, despite wondering about her motivation in writing to him with her news, given they hadn't seen each other for many years, and their only communication was her annual Christmas card. This was his *only* Christmas card, which was maybe why Noley—unfailingly sweet Noley—knowing this, had decided to write her letter to prepare him for the absence of her card that year or (worse still) for his shock at the receipt of a card signed by 'Noley & Ed'. He imagined good old Ed would even sign his own name as a gesture of seasonal solidarity. Noley would worry that Arthur might assume she were dead, or in some kind of trouble, if she didn't send a card. In a way this would be true, except any such assumption would only result in him crying briefly into his Christmas fare, after a buffet of alcoholic beverages, and feeling sorry for himself for a day or two, before rising from his crumpled, rather rancid bed to bugger on with his usual, self-serving aplomb.

Jealousy wasn't in Arthur's repertoire of emotions. He had usually tired of a woman before the news that she had found someone 'better' got in the way of things. Often it was a relief. However, an overriding sense of wrongness in his life, in this regard, characterised his latter-day attachment to a woman called Rini. She was so much younger, wiser and truly *better* than him in every way that even a vain old idiot like himself couldn't classify the daily pain he endured when she was in the company of people other than himself as jealousy. What he felt was abiding *regret*—not jealousy—that he hadn't been able to meet her when he was a younger, still passionate man yet possessed with an older man's reason and restraint; and a conviction that, if their stars had aligned, they might have been lovers. He once summoned enough Dutch courage to tell her as much, having persuaded her to spend a night out in the woods with him, a fire, and a borrowed dog. Humility came as easily as a breath in and a breath out for Rini Sanchez, and his words of flattery usually washed over her or made her smile. For her own part, she had only known first the fleeting affections of a man called Ben whom she'd felt duty bound to love; and was now navigating the attentions of a second man called Tam whose approach was as tentative as a night-fed hedgehog, curious to take what she offered yet nervous about how he might deal with the outcome of discovery. She declared she had no idea how she might have felt about a young Arthur Smith, who would most likely have been a sulky and opinionated young man if the senior incarnation was anything to go by; but she wasn't about to crush the fantasy of an old man whom she had grown to cherish so dearly in friendship, as well as by association with his grandson whom, she had to believe, he loved almost as much as she did.

Arthur decided to press Noley's letter between the pages of a book. As a graduate of English literature, he presided over a collection of books that, by their sheer number, made a mockery of anything else he had ever owned. He was often unable to lay his hands on a matching pair of socks, or a knife and fork, but he knew exactly where to find *A Midsummer Night's Dream*. His fingers traced the uneven spines of his bookshelves, and he counted to seventy—always his number of choice should a number require his choosing, as this was the number of the house he had once shared with his wife—and he landed upon *The Hand of Ethelberta* by Thomas Hardy, a book he could scarcely remember reading, which suggested it wasn't one of the author's finest. It stirred in him the recollection that it was about a woman's quest for a suitable match. This made Arthur grunt at the irony of where these literary chips had fallen, as he stowed Noley's letter firmly in the belly of the book, and set about preparing a breakfast for both himself and his spaniel friend.

Later that morning, he took the dog out into the woods, and tried to walk off what was in part a hangover, and, in another part, an ongoing obsession with his own demise that had plagued his imagination for far too much of his adult life. He watched Bryony-Brian's rear end bobbing through the undergrowth, and wondered who would take care of her should Steve's old lady not want her back, or if, indeed, he were to take her on and die whilst on duty. Duty was a confused concept for a man like Art, who had never been able to recognise it as a choice: it was either an obvious state of affairs (like going out of your way not to run someone over), or something he would reject point blank (like sending a Christmas card). It was only when he met Rini—who had opened up for him a Pandora's box of emotions—that he began to understand the mutual benefits that taking responsibility for others (human others) could bring. She saw gaps in the world that she imagined she might be able to fill, while he had only ever seen gaps that needed leaping over in case they turned out to be puddles deep enough to drown in. Most importantly, she had made sense of the connection between him and his only remaining family, but he remained at odds as to how he might do the boy any service, real service, before he died.

Arthur had battled with cancer, and was afraid that he would die of it. As an avid reader, he was determined that his last page would not depict him in a hospital bed surrounded by wires and monitors, his mouth hanging open like a cave caked with stalactites, and a humiliating paucity of grievers. He wanted to write his own final chapter.

Not unusually, he found himself pausing at the breach in the woods where he could step into the other world wherein he had met his wife, and subsequently left her to her horrible fate without him. He was tempted to take Bryony with him that day on a journey to see Rini, to crave her attention and compassion—despite her reticence to encourage him while her society continued to battle the scourge of a pandemic—but thought better of it.

He sat where he often sat with Rini, on the bench that marked the boundary between his world and hers. Bryony lay patiently at his feet once she had completed her exhaustive inventory of all the smells in the vicinity that he had restricted her to by bringing them to this unwelcome sit-still. His gaze fixed upon the tribe of brown, broken-skinned tree trunks in his midst, almost certainly the same ones whose company he had shared for the past half century, with the exception of those that had been sacrificed for the greater good of the forest, or mankind, or a conceptual muddle of both. His left eye began to twitch, at first intermittently, and then rather more persistently, and he marked that this had been happening a lot lately. Maybe he needed new glasses, or maybe it was an indication that he had done enough looking at trees for one lifetime. He experimented by opening and closing his eye to stop the twitching, but it didn't make any appreciable difference, like opening and closing his hands on a fluttering chick: it was still aflutter when released from his grip.

Bryony joined him in the forage for a bag of mushrooms for his lunch, and then they turned for home. Meandering away from the place he considered his gateway to Rini, he thought he heard the snapping of twigs underfoot that wasn't caused by his own boots. Bryony turned with him, an ear and a paw raised in anticipation of company, graciously convincing him that he wasn't imagining it. He half expected to see his brother-in-law approaching them in a state of consternation, but reason quickly reminded him that Dillan was now old and infirm, and wouldn't be walking the woods in search of his errant sister's useless husband anymore. Arthur chided himself (albeit without much conviction) for acknowledging that he was unlikely to ever come across Dillan again, and he was heartily glad of it.

He told Bryony that today was her lucky day. He was going to invest in a proper pair of poultry shears to make preparing her meals easier, and all the more rewarding to the human male side of the arrangement, as it required handling shiny metal and sharp blades. Arthur felt sure that nature had equipped the dog with a set of canine dentition that was more than up to the task of crunching bones, but he also knew she was more used to eating biscuits and tins of slop, so didn't want Steve visiting May with the news that Bryony had choked on a rabbit's foot. As this mission required a trip to David and Seth's shop (where he had endless credit), he was of a mind to invest in a new frying pan for the mushrooms, too, as his old one was warped and inefficient—and he recalled that the ironmonger's harboured a pleasing array of Teflon-coated cookware, hanging in orderly rows of kitchen armoury.

'The boys', as Arthur still called them, were not working that day, but he left Bryony in the capable care of the young woman behind the till who seemed pleased to have a distraction from unpacking boxes of light bulbs in order to hold the dog up at the window, and give her a commentary on what was going on outside on the street.

He couldn't find what he was looking for in the scissors department, as it seemed David and Seth's clientèle were targeted with garlic (not bone) crushers; but he did find a suitable pan that he enjoyed batting through the air for minute or two, before challenging himself to toss and catch it by the handle. He'd assumed he was alone and unseen, until a woman's laughter interrupted his antics, and almost caused him to drop the pan, which would have suffered the same denting as his pride.

'So you've taken up tennis in your old age?'

He turned to see Noley, a generation (surely) older: her trademark halo of curls now shorn and highlighted to favour the greys, her habitual array of ear and nose rings replaced with simple studs and a neat necklace.

'Your letter,' was all he could say in the moment.

'Oh, yes,' she said, and coyly proffered her left hand, that she wiggled to indicate an engagement ring. 'I thought you might like to know.'

'But you're here?' he said, wondering, more than anything, what the point of posting the letter had been if she had intended a visit.

'I am,' she said. 'I nearly didn't come, but I had some loose ends to tie up.'

'After all this time?' he said. He had his pan, and she had a handful of random items that seemed to include seed packets and labels for jam jars.

'After all this time!'

'So, *congratulations*,' said Arthur, jabbing his pan handle at the word, to indicate he had remembered social nicety.

'Thank you, Art,' said Noley. 'And you? Did you ever find your Mrs Smith?'

She smiled and looked around for evidence of a wife who might have been cowering by the bags of compost.

'Mrs...? Oh, no,' said Art. 'That ship has long since sailed and run aground.'

She looked at him askance, amused, as though she wanted to press him for more meaning, but felt obliged to keep their conversation light. He realised he had probably spoken out of turn, and wanted to leave.

'I have mushrooms to cook for lunch,' he said, adding hastily, 'For a friend, so... It's been nice, extraordinary, to see you.'

Noley shook her head as though she had expected no more from this chance meeting, but was glad she had seen him.

'I did a double-take when I saw the scarf,' she ventured to say, nodding at Arthur's chest. His 'bandit' scarf, the one he had conceded to wear when on Rini's side, hung loosely thereabouts. He had picked it up from a charity shop (in fact he might have helped himself to it whilst walking *past* a charity shop), and he registered that the pattern of multi-coloured skulls was probably not something that Noley would have envisaged him wearing when they had been together.

'No, it's not one I wear often,' he said, although the truth was that these days he was never without it, in case he found himself away from home, and about to be scolded by Rini for not covering his nose and mouth. 'It's really only high days and holidays…'

With gratifying canine intuition that a rescue might be required, Bryony began to bark herself out of the till-girl's favour, so was released, and she leapt to the floor, and scampered to Arthur's side. There was no further need to make small talk, as Noley had leaned over and kissed him, squeezing his pan-free hand, and taken hasty leave of the shop where they had once worked together, clutching her small stash of items.

Hardly a *trousseau*, he reflected later, as he tried to make sense of their strange and final meeting.

Before he managed to get round to cooking his mushrooms, Arthur was distracted by half a bottle of shiraz that sent him to sleep in his kitchen chair. He dreamt he was eating ceps that he had picked in the French countryside with a brown-skinned woman, but whenever he turned to see her face it became lost in the trunks of trees that seemed to want to consume her, and deny him. He woke himself with a loud, jaw-cracking snort that brought Bryony anxiously up onto his lap for reassurance that she wasn't, yet again, at risk of mortal danger in his custody. He apologised and smoothed down her ears, telling himself that, just like his twitching eye, his tendency to fall asleep during the day was becoming a regular occurrence, as was waking up gasping for air, like a sheet of newspaper had blown into his face when he had been a boy cycling home from school, inducing then—as it did now—the fear of suffocation, collision, and death.

110

'Just a dream,' he told Bryony, who was hopeful that the rustling of the mushroom bag might mean something good would be coming her way too.

He lamented that a dream of being a young man sharing ceps with the woman he loved was about to be supplanted by a mere plate of mushrooms on toast with someone else's dog.

Bryony began to bark again, as though she shared his disappointment. As he turned away from his new pan that was proudly spitting butter, he realised she was barking at something else, something very real and present. It was the opening of his kitchen door and the entry of a boy who looked to Arthur like he was staring death in the face sooner than *he* was, either in his imagination or in reality.

It was his grandson Torran.

DEE (II)

Before she took her coffee out into the ice-cold morning air, Dee D'Abruzzo checked on her young companion who remained unconscious in the small spare room. She was shrouded in a duvet the same colour as the heather that clung to the landscape outside of their cabin. This pleased Dee, as it felt like appropriate attention to detail by whoever had attended to the interior design of the place. She approved of a job well done.

A teenager's ability to sleep late into the day had always mystified her. She understood the science behind the biology and psychology—of the 'second development stage of cognitive maturation'—but it was something she had never experienced herself. She had always been an early riser, even on mornings when she woke up feeling as though it might have been preferable to descend under the covers for an hour or two longer—to sink back into sleep, or to seek pleasure in the stimulation of her private parts. She was generally on her guard for whoever else might be awake before her (usually this was her twin sister Demmy), and whether it might be wiser for her to be up and active before the rest of the household beat her to it.

It was only seven thirty, however, so she had no qualms in closing the door gently on this particular teenager's slumber, and padding silently away in her warm, woollen socks. She shook down the heaviness from her arms that were unused to lifting the type of 'luggage' she'd arrived with the previous evening.

She would set an alarm to remind herself to check on the girl (her niece) in an hour or so. How long she should leave it before becoming 'concerned' was something she wasn't clear about. Demmy hadn't thought to give her opinion on that, given most of her sister's knowledge about the effects of the new wonder drug she was so keen to champion appeared limited to the rodent population.

A fleeting vision of her sister's face troubled her momentarily: paler than usual (on account of her horror) against the fire of her hair, that was doing its usual job of obliterating the face of anyone else in her midst—in this instance that of her husband Ben, as they rallied together in the terrible realisation of the consequences of fast-tracking an untried and untested drug. A *breakthrough* drug, in essence: the global success of which Demmy had hoped to take a good deal of the credit for herself.

Dee took a deep breath, inhaling the aroma of freshly ground coffee beans, and the invigorating, woody scent of the outdoors; and thought about remorse. How would she deal with it, if it did actually manifest itself in her, as it wasn't something she was familiar with. *Regret*, perhaps, at a missed opportunity, or someone else's foolishness, but not really *remorse*, or pity, or guilt.

She closed her eyes on the morning, and sunlight cut through the chill air off the water to bathe her face in the serenity of her lakeside retreat. She shouldn't clutter her mind with uncertainty, but bask in *certainty*— that which would definitely come to pass, because she herself had been the engineer.

Less than an hour earlier, Dee had pressed 'send' on the key of her laptop so that, soon after, she imagined (*almost* certainly) that Professor James Whatton, her former boss and mentor, would have interrupted his breakfast—or curtailed his morning run, or postponed the sexual service of Mrs Whatton—to take stock of her arresting news. This would be even more distracting than the revelation that his laboratory had been staffed with errant idiots who had seen fit to cook up recreational drugs on his careless watch. *This* would stop him in his tracks, not least as she had copied in professors at every other laboratory they had dealt with when they'd worked together.

'*Dear Professor Whatton,*' she had written. '*Up until this morning, you will only remember me (if you remember me at all) as the sister of Demmy D'Abruzzo. I am Dee D'Abruzzo, whom you conspired to remove from your laboratory on the grounds that I was a poor fit for your team. It would appear that you made a wise move (for me, at any rate) as I went on to work elsewhere, where my talents were recognised by the research programme that formulated the Virid20 vaccine. Should you have been following my career more closely than that of my sister, however, you won't be aware that she has been extremely busy in Geneva, striving to be at the forefront of ground-breaking research into what she (and the wider world of science, perhaps) likes to believe will be the elixir of life. I doubt you will be privy to much information about this, as I understand it is classified, unless I do your professional standing, these days, a disservice. I can confirm that I, myself, know very little apart from the fact it is currently at kill or cure status (not very scientific, even by your questionable standards), but I have been charged to test it out on the human population. Quite a responsibility—or should I call it a privilege? My sister seems to have more faith in me than you did. The challenge (or rather, my challenge) has been to procure human subjects from the Curator population who would neither be missed nor mourned should they fall foul of the research programme—and by that, Professor, I mean should they have been killed, by me, in the name of progress. More specifically (and it was ever thus) for my sister's progress.*

I want you to know the truth about my situation, as a scientist as well as a sister.

I was faithful to my task in finding a 'suitable' young man; once Demmy followed through with supplying me with phials of her wonder drug. Twenty of them in total. I marvel at her confidence that her inferior twin sister would be able to both access twenty members of the underclass, and also be prepared to commit what would likely amount to mass murder. And make no mistake, Professor, this is what I am telling you: my sister is a murderer.

At this point, I urge you to stop reading, and endeavour to put to her (and her team) the following questions:

Is there an antidote?

Have any of her sleepy mice been resuscitated?

While you are at it, you might like to tell her that I have had limited success with my sample. Namely only two subjects to date. The first, a boy named Torran Smith who would have gone like a lamb to the slaughter had I not taken pity on him. He asked for cash upfront, and I gave it to him, from what my sister had seen fit to deposit into my bank account in the guise of 'funding my research'—a bribe, to all intents and purposes (the type of transaction I'm sure you, and certainly my former colleagues at your laboratory, might be familiar with).

I don't expect to see him again, and good luck to him. Although he may need encouragement to keep his mouth shut. I will leave that to those who might give a damn.

However, my second subject is a work in progress. She is my niece Lora, who is currently sleeping soundly in my spare room. She didn't object to my invitation to supper—in fact she seemed rather pleased to be asked, and to drink rather a lot of my excellent wine, as her parents 'don't allow it'. This was our secret. Well, one of them. The other was that I intended to use her as part of her mother's drug trial—without her consent, of course, as I didn't imagine she would be tempted by the same financial incentive as the boy. Too smart to play a game of chance with her own life, however, so I decided to do it for her: to sedate her (in fact I have sedated her twice), and to bring her with me on my trip to the north.

This morning I have also injected her with one of the phials. To make our family's 'research' all the more interesting, I made it a truly blind sample. I created my own placebo (or, rather, I used my very own Virid20 vaccine!), mixed up both the live and placebo shots, and picked at random.

So, Professor, Demmy, Ben (and the rest of you so-called scientists), it remains to be seen whether the first 'human' Genevieve will stir from slumber, and go on to live forever, or sink away into unsuspecting martyrdom.

Lora may become one of the most famous women in history, or be just another victim of an infamous mother. It's nothing if not intriguing.

I remain curious. How long do I leave it before I try to rouse her?

This, of all times, is the time to take note of my work.

I look forward to hearing from you.

With professional regards,

Dee D'Abruzzo

JADE

Sirius, or Siria, I'll call it, no matter what anyone else thinks. No matter what *he* says, although I think he'll let me call it whatever I please. He's like that: pleasing me is what he seems to like more than anything else.

Daft thing is, he isn't even sure he's the father. I'm OK with him not knowing that he's actually the only bloke that I've ever gone the whole way with without a wrap on. He's the sweetest kiddy, and it spices my blood knowing he's that into me.

I won't get rid of it, like some desperate Dispo. It's what my mum did, time and again, until I came along and somehow managed to hang on inside her while the rest of them got flushed away. I'm a special kid, I am. He reckons he had it tough with his junkie mother: mine just bred me with the lady-balls to get on and survive. *'Jade, you're a warrior'*, she says. *'A survivor'*. In this world, you've got to be.

Don't get me wrong, I've had my dives. Lockdown was the pits, and made those of us with pretty miserable lots even more depressed. It strikes me that when everyone is on a downer, it's them that aren't used to it that bleat the most and take advantage of bad times. I had mates who couldn't get fixed up without taking backhanders from the Council, high and mighty bastards who use and abuse for their own gains whilst making out they are pillars of the community. They think they're unseen, but we know who they are, and their judgement day will come. It wasn't Mr Reggie Sanchez who was caught painting hate graffiti on some random's door, but it was him handing over the cash to my cousin Jez and his mate to get it done. I was the look-out, and I'd been looking out with my camera! My mum says it pays to know whose governor the nearest Governor is, and one of these days there might be some shit hitting a fan very close to our man Reggie.

Makes me want to laugh and punch the air.

My kiddy Torran has had his share of scrapes, but lately he's been talking about getting a proper job at the laboratory where they test all sorts of shit on animals. Turns my stomach (although that could just be 'cos of me being knocked up), but I reckon it might be a good thing if it gives us steady money. We're going to need it. I always thought he was one of the Parkinsons, but it turned out they weren't his real family, and neither was the woman he got to know at the lab. Thick as thieves he is with her: it seems there's been quite a queue of dickheads willing to take him on!

Cute as hell, mind. When he laughs he's got such a big gap in his teeth you can fit a roll-up in it, and the maddest curly hair that I swear one day's going to break my scissors! Something about him makes my heart hurt, though, but in a good way. I hope the baby's as cute, and not some bald little baboon like Jez's kid.

I feel bad for not telling my mum everything about Torran and me. You have to be careful who you trust (*she* taught me that), and I don't think I can trust her about the money. It's more money than I'd ever seen in one stash. Don't ask, he said, but I had to do some digging. *'I can't put the baby in danger'*, I said, so he told me he'd conned a Governor, but he had a plan to get away with it. I must be getting soft in pregnancy, because I told him I'd go along with it.

Little did I know what he was letting me in for.

He came for me as the sun was going down, told me to pack a bag with only the stuff I couldn't live without, and, of course, the money. I thought better of telling him I could live without everything except him and his kid. He took me into the woods and made me put on a blindfold, told me that he was taking me back to his grandfather's, but the old man insisted I wasn't to know the way there, or the way back, for my own safety. It was odd as fuck, him steering me through trees that smelled of damp and decay and fox shit, not knowing where the hell I was going. His grandfather had given him his old coat to wear which might have been where the smell of fox shit came from. I grabbed onto his thick, waxy arm, and did as I was told. I figured there were times when even a warrior needed guiding.

I was allowed to take off my blindfold when we arrived in his grandfather's garden. I heard Torran force open a heavy gate to let us in, and I followed him into the old man's kitchen. I recognised him as the old bugger who used to wander round our streets with a fancy scarf tied around his face, who I'd imagined was just some Dispo from the arse-end of town.

So this was Art, another player from Torran's life who looked out for him, but this one from the shadows. His ratty little black and white dog leapt up at my belly, so I knocked it away.

'She won't do you any harm,' the old man said, all funny, but lifted the dog off by its collar. 'Her name's Bryony, but I call her Brian.'

'I'm Jade,' I said.

'I know, and I'm Arthur, but you can call me Art,' he said. 'Welcome to your new home.'

*

By the time Torran's woman friend from the lab arrived, Art had made us toast and eggs, and cups of strong tea. He offered me mushrooms that I refused to eat because they smelled rank, and I didn't want to put my baby at risk. The old man laughed and told me that Torran's grandmother had eaten the same mushrooms before she fell pregnant with his mum Angelica.

Yeah, and she turned out mad, I thought to myself, but didn't say anything to anyone.

Rini had turned up late enough to avoid the offer of mushrooms, and didn't seem to have much appetite for anything else. She was relieved to see Torran and hugged him for longer than he or I would have liked. I wanted to pull her off, not because I was jealous, but because I wanted to spare him his embarrassment. This was a new feeling for me, wanting to look out for him.

'Do we have to stay here?' I asked him, on the quiet. 'I mean, where the hell are we?'

Torran said nothing, and now Rini had turned up he seemed tired and scared. It gave me the jitters.

Arthur poured large glasses of red wine for everyone, which pissed me off, as Torran had already told him about the baby. I got up and emptied mine down the sink.

'I want to go home,' I said, and squared up. 'Torran, I want you to take me home.'

Art drank. Rini moved her glass round in circles. Torran ran his hands through his mad mop of hair.

'We can't go home,' he said. '*I* can't go home.'

'It's just a bit of knocked off cash,' I snapped. 'I can cover for you, for a bit. For as long as it takes. And no one's going to come looking for *me*.'

The silence in the kitchen was eventually broken by the dog sitting up sharp and scratching behind its ear like something possessed.

'You can't take that risk, Jade,' said Rini. I wanted to fly at her, but she had the sort of stillness about her that settled my nerves. Of the three of them, she seemed the sanest; and the fact they allowed her into their confidence gave me hope, despite myself. I let her take me by the arm and bring me back to my seat beside her. 'The way things are, Torran will be in trouble, and it won't take the authorities long to come looking for you. We need to think about what's best for you and the baby.'

'She can go home, if she wants to,' said Torran, calmly. 'I can look out for her. She doesn't have to leave everything behind.'

'And what if you don't?' said Art, bringing his hand down heavily onto the table. He had polished off his glass already, and his cheeks were on fire with wine. 'What if, like me, you think you can come and go, until the coming becomes too much for you, and you stop? And you never see Jade or your daughter again?'

'We don't know it's a girl,' I said, crossly, but glad the kid was part of the conversation, bringing something less fucked up into it. Rini shook her head gently at me, and refilled his glass.

'Torran isn't *you*, Art,' she said. 'He has my support, for one thing. He can lie low for as long as it takes, and I can keep an eye out for Jade.'

'My Rini,' said Art, with what seemed like gratitude for her words as well as for the wine. The dog, deciding it preferred the old man's lap to its basket, jumped up, settled down, and eyed us all like unwanted guests. 'However, he has a choice that I never had. A home of his own, for one thing. A bag of cash, which, to be honest, will be spent in no time on nappies and such, but there *will* be a not insubstantial inheritance.'

'So you expect us to live here with you until you croak?' I said, my tongue suddenly taken over by wickedness.

Torran winced; Rini just closed her eyes.

'I do,' said Art, smilingly. 'And you won't have long to wait.'

*

I couldn't believe he'd sprung me into this hell-hole. I found the smallest place to hide—a cupboard under the stairs—crept in and sat hugging my knees and my baby close. Rini found me when I was just about ready to pee my pants, so I let her coax me out.

I'd seen it. She had a bag of needles and shit with her. All the stuff she reckoned she needed to see the old bastard off. They were in it together, including Torran, and it was the most fucked up thing I'd ever heard of. He wanted her to give him a lethal injection, and we were supposed to go along with it, keeping our mouths shut, so we could take on his house in this back of beyond secret garden, his *gift to his family*, and tell no one!

It was doing my head in. I'd never wanted a fix so bad since I'd found out I was knocked up, and I hated them for it. I'm no cry baby, but things got the better of me. I got myself into a bit of a screaming mess, and she had to take me in hand. She wrapped me in a blanket and made me tea: not his stinking black brew, but something sweeter that calmed me down. I had a kip on the sofa, with the dog at my feet. It was quite nice, in the end, like it was keeping watch over me.

'No one's saying we can't *never* go back, Jay,' Torran said, later. He was more serious than I'd ever seen him. Maybe it was the dad coming out in him. 'But we'd need to let things settle down, 'cos of the money, and 'cos I don't know what I've got caught up in. And no one can find us here, not unless they really know what they are looking for...'

'How did *you* get here?' I asked.

'I followed my grandad. I'd followed him before and could see him disappearing in the woods. It seemed kind of mad, but I needed to know where he was going, and I needed him to help me. It was easy enough if I kept on his tail, 'cos there's a space by an old bench which is like a crossing. Rini says this is a whole other world.'

I tried to take all this in.

'So we'd be *free?*' I said, a bit stupidly, after a moment or two. His hand was close and I touched his fingers with mine.

'Yeah,' he laughed. 'We'd have our own place. He reckons he's already given the house over to his mate Steve, in *trust* for us. And our time has come to have it.'

I didn't like the thought of trusting anyone except him, but didn't say it.

'Will we fit in?' I asked. I'd never lived anywhere else apart from my mum's shitty little house that we shared with two other families. Even though Art's gaff was no palace, and smelled like old people and cabbage, it was better than anything I'd ever imagined for myself, or for the kid.

'We're not so different,' said Torran, grinning so I could see that great gap in his choppers. 'We'll get the measure of things in no time, you wait and see.'

'I could still have the baby at home, though, back home, where I'm used to?' I said, although I'd been cheered up by his confidence.

'Yeah, I reckon so,' he said. 'Things will have calmed down by then. And Rini will know what to do, and who to work on if needs be.'

'Just promise me you won't leave us, like he did,' I said. 'You'll come back for us?'

'I promise,' he said. 'Course I promise.'

I wondered if his grandad had said the same to his grandmother in the commune all them years ago. What made him, Torran, so different? I reckon it was probably her, Rini—she's got some way with her, she has.

'Is it true what the old man said.' I went on. 'He met your grandmother on our side of things, and just abandoned her?'

'Yeah. He can be a slippery sod.'

'Well, I'm glad you're not like him.'

'I am like him sometimes,' he said, taking a big, brave breath. 'Which is why he wants things to be different for me.'

I didn't want to move my fingers away from his, not ever.

'Let's be different, then,' I said.

*

She couldn't promise it was going to be all plain sailing. She said she knew how much stuff was needed to stop the heart of a mouse or a rabbit, but she'd never had to finish off a grown man before. He was proper laid back about it; he said he'd done his research, and between them, between us, we'd do alright.

She said his mate Steve would be coming the next day to pick up Brian, and we were to give him a letter from Art, telling him the time had come, and what was what. She reckoned no one would miss him, or ask awkward questions, and that she and Steve would know what to do with 'the body', afterwards, back on our side. There might be a woman he'd been shacked up with in the past come looking for him, but we just had to tell her he'd moved on. Which he would have.

Looking at the mad old scrote getting more and more oiled at his kitchen table, I couldn't help feeling that we *were* all in it together, and we were giving him (my kid's great-grandfather!) the send-off that he wanted, before an even shittier ending maybe got the better of him.

I just wish that I didn't keep getting leaky-eyed like some daft kid.

'I don't want you to be afraid,' Rini said to me. 'There's someone I need to speak to tonight, but I'll be back to meet Steve, and to take care of Art. You mustn't worry about anything.'

'Is it your soppy cat-man?' I said, 'cos I'd heard stories from Torran, who reckoned he had the hots for her.

'I suppose you could say that,' she said, with the faintest of blushes. 'It's time he knew the truth.'

'About this?!' I said.

'Not all of it,' she said. 'Not yet. But one day.'

I made myself scarce when they decided it was time to get the old man into his bed. They'd set it up in the downstairs room, to make it easier, she said, to remove his body when the time came. They helped him undress and put on comfortable kit to sleep in. To die in.

'I might shit myself,' he said, slyly, to his grandson. 'A small price to pay, eh?'

Rini rolled her eyes, and tried to hide the fact she was probably terrified. He must have done quite a job on her to get her to agree to this. Torran told me later they had the craziest friendship: that they connected because she was a truly *good* person and he, well *he* had spent all his life trying fucking hard to be one, and maybe hoped some of it would finally rub off.

Was this him being the best he could be, some goodness rubbing off? I wondered, when I dared put my head around the door, and watched as his breathing began to slow down and crackle. After all, he was giving his life for me, and Torran, and little Siria. This was going to be our new start, which, despite scaring the shit out of me, was *pretty* fucking good!

It's what he believed. It's what we all wanted to believe as we watched him die, the crazy old bastard.

He struggled a bit like he was seeing something he didn't want to see before he finally croaked.

She held his head in her arms like she was carrying him over. I wept another bucket.

RINI (III)

It was dusk when Rini was making her way back through Arthur's woodland to the breach that would take her home to rest, to organise her thoughts, and to plan her return for his body.

The vision of his pallid, death-drawn face and those of the youngsters—Jade's a mask of blatant fear and disgust, Torran's set with the same grim determination he had learned to copy from his grandfather—rattled her resolve a little, but she would remain true to her task, for the sake of them all.

What if we fail? she had asked Art, at one point.

He had replied, with satisfaction at his cleverness at appropriating one of his many quotes for the occasion: *'Then we fail. But screw your courage to the sticking place, and we'll not fail.'*

All the creatures who had met their end at her fingertips, all the rabbits and mice, seemed to dart and dance out of her way as she brushed past trees, shrugging off the low-reaching branches that sought to detain her. She would not be detained. She would not let dark thoughts unsettle her now she had turned her hand to taking the life of an old man. It had been his will, and, of all of her charges, he had been the one with a choice. The others had met their fate at the will of Governors who demanded their deaths to understand more about life. But it was too late to question any of it now.

She faltered at the breach, as the fading light was not in her favour, and she realised she had never passed through at this time of the evening before. She had never crossed alone: she had always had him next to her or at her heels, or waiting on the other side. Her heart fluttered at the loss of him, but she pushed on, knowing she was doing his bidding. Then she stumbled, and became aware that she wasn't where she had expected to be: a habitually patient person, she felt uncharacteristically frustrated and angry at this impasse. There was so much at stake, she needed to make haste for the sake of the youngsters. She got to her feet to find herself back down on her knees, then tumbling forwards into the undergrowth, like she had been turned and shoved in a game of blindfolded trickery by Becks or Reggie when they'd been children. For a few terrifying seconds she kept falling, until she landed with a bump at the base of a tree, the gigantic roots both breaking her fall and challenging the imposition of her clumsy arrival. She scrabbled to her feet and wrapped her arms around its mighty girth, peering up into a canopy of leaves that seemed to be filtering through more light than the hour of the day had been affording her just moments earlier.

Rini was lost.

With her back to the trunk of the tree, she wondered what she was going to do. Who could help her now? She thought of Art, and of Tam: the only people who had shown her any real compassion or tenderness since the death of her parents. What would they do? Her eyes pricked with tears that she dissolved with a sniff as soon as she felt them try their luck.

Find the path. It won't be an obvious path, but you will notice it's where the ground is more downtrodden, not necessarily in a straight line, it might be a zig zag, a broken line, but it's there if you look for it, it's where the deer and foxes and stupid old men who should be at home with wives and wine will have walked before you. Follow the path.

Thank you, Art.

She began to pick her way through the layer of roots to where she was convinced of a pathway.

She thought of Tam. She needed more reassurance.

Just come back safe, Rini.

Rini's face relaxed into a smile, despite her predicament. She walked for what must have been half an hour before the woodland was split in half by a narrow track. One way or the other, she decided, she would find a signpost that would direct her to the neighbourhood she knew to be either Art's or her own, and she would simply need to start her journey again. She refused to be afraid.

She turned left onto the track—she was left-handed, so it was a decision made easily by her, maybe *for* her—and picked up a confident pace, only slightly nonplussed by the gradual dimming of daylight around her that had, surely, been all but extinguished an hour ago. Could she have slipped somewhere between the layers of Art's world and her own, where the time she had left and the time she had arrived were slightly at odds with each other? She began to walk more quickly as a sense of foreboding rose in her chest—the faster she walked, the more she could put her racing heart down to speed and not her mounting agitation.

Help me, Art.

She kept walking until she feared she might throw up. She had no water; she didn't dare get any more dehydrated than she might be already.

Help me.

Nothing.

Rini stopped and looked left and right into the blackening bodies of trees, closing in on each other as darkness fell, dismissing her desire for sanctuary and denying her more clues as to where her road home might be. The forest was no help to her now.

I've found the path, Art. But where does it lead? Which way am I headed?

Despite her lifelong ambition to be brave, resourceful, a saviour, Rini Sanchez felt tears of desperation and fear start to stream down her face, etching itchy lines through dirt and sweat. Her concern was no longer for Art, Torran, or Jade. She was afraid for herself. She sank into the undergrowth at the side of the road and wept, hugging her knees to her chest for warmth and comfort, daring herself not to shiver too much in order to cheat the chill of nightfall, and to conserve her energy for the morning. Oh, morning! She had never wished so hard for a new day to dawn in all her life. Her tears kept falling despite her dragging them away with the back of her hand, just like Torran when he refused to give in to life's injustices. She suddenly felt like her heart was pouring out a lifetime of grief: for the loss of her parents, of Joe, and of her sweet, unborn baby daughter.

And for Tam, whom she feared she might never see again.

Darkness, numbness. Rini slept or lost consciousness, she couldn't be sure which until she was awoken by someone pulling her up from her shoulders. Someone strong and familiar.

'Where in Deiman's name have you been? We've been looking everywhere for you! And what are you wearing? Beg pardon, milady.'

It was Clem, standing over her, with what appeared to be a horse drawn carriage a little way behind. Clem in a garment with a tightly laced bodice and long flowing skirt, fingerless gloves made of stiff and dirty fabric. Clem with two strong arms and a flushed face that was both relieved and cross in the same moment.

'Where am I, Clem?' said Rini, her tear-wretched voice coming out as a rasp. 'How did you find me? Can you help me get home?'

'You bet I can, milady, or my life won't be worth a sack of acorns!'

'A sack of—?'

'Swine food, milady.' Clem fastened her arm (still, Rini was fascinated by its proximity to another, fully functioning arm) around her waist and steered her to the carriage where a black horse champed on its bridle and nodded an unintentional greeting. The driver stepped down from his seat in readiness to get them moving.

'Found her, then?' he said. Rini was looking at a grey-faced man in a loose shirt and leathers whose resting expression was a gold-garnished sneer—where there wasn't gold there were broken black teeth, the jagged smile of the dispossessed 'Not looking so high and mighty today is she, His Favourite!?'

'That's enough from you, Archie,' said Clem, with an attitude that gave Rini a surge of hope. She almost swooned into Clem's embrace until she realised it was merely the means to secure her, and shove her up the two steps into the carriage. 'You can keep your idle chat for those that give a squit. Just get us back, and sharp.'

Rini found herself in a surprisingly well-appointed interior, with thickly quilted walls and a double layer of curtains that Clem pulled shut and secured with wooden poles.

'He will overstep the mark, milady, we can't be too careful.'

She drew a leather bottle of water and pieces of bread from her pockets that Rini accepted with enthusiasm.

'Why are you talking to me like this, Clem? It's only me, Rini...'

Her friend was either not hearing her or choosing not to listen. Clem pulled a trunk out from beneath her seat and snapped open the clasp. She shook out a voluminous velvet dress, with a bodice like the one she was wearing herself, and began to loosen the laces.

'A change of clothes. I know, I think of everything. Don't I always?'

Rini looked on in astonishment. Despite the confusion of her situation, she was no longer lost and alone, and she was in the company of her dear old friend, albeit in a somewhat different form. At some point, this pretence would end and she would acknowledge her. Surely.

'You *were* always resourceful, Clem,' she ventured to say. 'I remember when you used to manage with one arm. Do you remember?'

Her words sounded absurd, even rude, in the strange confined space where they found themselves, and Clem reddened with discomfort.

'You aren't yourself, milady,' she said. 'Talking of such things. You must have breathed the night vapours of the forest, running away like you did. Let me help get you changed out of those slaving clothes and into your dress. I made sure it was His favourite. We can wash your face once we've got you back, and He'll be none the wiser.'

'Clem, I don't belong here,' said Rini, as the carriage rattled on, and they heard the driver coughing up phlegm at intervals and spitting it out into the morning mist. 'I'm caught between two worlds. I need you to help me to get back where I belong. Where we both belong! You are a scientist, Clem, not a lady's maid!'

'He said you could talk like a marsh sprite when the mood took you, milady, but I won't pay it any mind. Where you don't belong is the *gutter*, not any more, not while I have breath in my body.'

'Did I come from the gutter, Clem? Where did you come from? Where are we going?'

Clem laughed and began to undress her friend, her mistress, who could do nothing but lift her arms, and shift in her seat to allow her clothes to be removed, and replaced with velvet and lace. Resistance of any kind seemed pointless.

'He's losing patience, milady. There's talk. We pray you won't disappoint Him. We couldn't bear going back to how it was before you came.'

Rini sensed there was a lot riding on her comportment from now on, for her own salvation, and for that, suddenly, of countless others. In these bizarre circumstances, she began to feel like her old self.

'Is he a good man? A good Governor?' she asked. 'What do you think, Clem?'

'He's the king,' said Clem, simply, and smiled the smile Rini remembered as the one she reserved for her announcements that she had aced her grades again.

'I see.' Clem was fussing with sleeves and a lop-sided neckline, so Rini smoothed her skirts and played her part. 'And what does he want from me, in your opinion?'

'I don't ought to have an opinion, milady.'

'But if I were to ask, as a friend?'

'Begging pardon, we aren't friends,' said Clem, a little stubbornly. 'Milady.'

'Well, what if I command you, as your king's favourite,' said Rini. 'What would your opinion be then?'

Clem sat back in her seat and examined the hands in her lap that were dry and overworked.

'He wants what we all want.'

'I want to go home,' said Rini, more urgently. 'I want to bury my dear friend, and make sure his grandchildren will be safe. And I want to tell someone that I love them, too.'

'Then you best tell Him what he wants to hear. His future. How He will be remembered as the greatest king we've ever known. Then maybe we'll all have a chance at happiness.'

'Is he that big-headed?!' Rini laughed.

'His crown is big,' Clem replied, without irony.

'Why is it so important for you to know your future, Clem? Why should you trust me to tell you that?'

'You were right about the plague, milady. You saw it coming and you saved our lives, well, as many lives as you could. Your infirmary cherished the old who couldn't help but give themselves up to it, but it kept the rest of us from Deiman's door. You were our angel on earth.'

Clem paused as though she had just made a speech she had never planned to utter out loud, and certainly not to her saviour.

'I can't imagine it was all my own work,' said Rini, carefully.

'Your poor sainted father, Deiman save his soul,' said Clem. 'He built it with his own bare hands, mostly, it was said. It never seemed right that he was taken so young. He must rest happy knowing you are now the king's favourite, and our kingdom is safe in your hands.'

Rini must have looked unsettled, such that her friend said, 'Pardon, milady, your questions made me forget myself.'

'No matter,' said Rini. 'I was glad to hear you talk of such things. The night's adventure must have made *me* forget myself.'

The two women sat in silence then until the carriage came to a sudden stop. Clem had been dozing with her head against the door, but she leapt up as the horse's hooves struck a heavy standstill on cobblestones, and she pulled back the wooden guard and curtains in order for them to alight.

Rini found herself at the gates of an imposing, fortified building. A castle, of course. They were admitted without the driver who was sent elsewhere with the horse and carriage, and Clem ushered Rini in through a side door, along a series of corridors and up stone staircases to what she assumed must be her own rooms.

'When was I here last?' she asked, looking around in wonder at the large canopied bed, the wood panelled walls, oil lamps, and coarse-woven rugs. The paintings on the walls were of stern-faced women with children glaring out from the confines of overly ornate frames, and bleak landscapes.

'I tended to you yesterday before you took your leave,' said Clem, archly. She filled a basin with water and splashed it with her hands. 'Hot it isn't, but it's clean. Shall I help you today, milady?'

'Yesterday?' said Rini. 'You won't believe what has happened between yesterday and today. You might think of it as the musings of a marsh sprite, or a soothsayer, but it's been a lifetime in another world, Clem.' She shook her head, wresting the cloth from Clem's exasperated grip to wash her own face. 'We were best friends, and you were the cleverest person I knew. I loved you so much.'

There was an urgent tap at the door, and Clem was relieved to abandon her uncomfortable position at Rini's side to admit another nervous looking woman who spoke in whispers, and left as hurriedly as she'd arrived.

'He's been asking for you all night, milady, you can't keep Him waiting any longer,' said Clem. 'Come along with me, do you remember the shortcut?'

'I don't.'

'Be quick about it, and don't be telling Him stories about your daydreams, if I may press upon your good opinion of me. He will only want to hear stories about Himself.'

Rini felt courage rising in her breast as she followed Clem through the darker passages of the castle to where the walls were more liberally decorated with blackened oil lamps and coats of arms. She spotted shields and crossed swords, imagining that historically (if not currently) her king had presided over armies of men. Perhaps he had been a soldier himself.

Art had told her stories of a king who had six wives, two of whom he beheaded. Wasn't there also a tale of a woman who was obliged to tell the king a story every night to spare her life? Kings, as far as Rini understood it, were the worst sort of Governors. She had never before been afraid in the company of a Governor, however, so she wasn't about to lose her nerve today, despite the timidity of the others she had encountered in this 'kingdom'.

A pair of guards stood either side of a heavy wooden door. Rini made out engravings of trees, and children gathering fruit from a forest floor in the company of small agile dogs. There were couples reclining in beds of leaves, reading books or (if her eyes weren't deceiving her) copulating. She had moments to process these images before the two halves of the door were laboriously parted to admit her, her head turning briefly to check that Clem was still at her side, but discovering her maid and erstwhile friend had disappeared.

She proceeded into the vast interior where she resisted the visceral urge to look up into a dome of sun-glittering glass way above her head, as this was not what she had been summoned to see. This must be the very top of the castle. The door sighed shut behind her. The king stood in her midst, consuming her attention, his back to her with hands clasped over the buttocks of his breeches. The wooden furnishings and effects of her bedroom were re-imagined around him in a more grandiose style: there were bookcases crammed with volumes scaling the walls, and sumptuously upholstered couches. He turned around slowly as he sensed her arrival, and reached out for a crystal decanter on the table at his elbow that could have seated twenty people, but was set with goblets, chargers, and knives and forks for just two.

'Rini, did you really think your world was the only one?'

These words resounded in her head as she took in the face and form of Art, her curmudgeonly old friend into whom she believed she had administered a fatal injection the evening before. At least he looked like Art, just as Clem had looked like Clem—only this was an entirely different reality.

'Will you make a habit of testing the patience of a king?' he asked, and poured wine while he awaited her reply.

'I wasn't aware it was a test,' she said.

'Where have you been?' he added, sharply. 'I have asked your women, and not one of them has been capable of coming up with anything resembling the truth.' He pushed a goblet firmly towards her with a defiant finger, ringed with gold and a large red jewel.

'I needed to clear my mind, sir. I spent time amongst the trees. I had no idea my absence would be so…'

'Incomprehensible? So infuriating?!' The king took a deep draught of wine. '*Drink* with me, Deiman damn you, now you are here.'

'Yes, sir.' Rini stepped forward and took her goblet, taking a small sip.

'Drink! And I am no *sir*! I am your *majesty!*'

'You know I don't have your stomach for wine. Your majesty.'

He poured himself more, and scowled at the glass she cradled against her bodice.

'It is said you have more time for the lion tamer than you do for your king,' he said, with an air of sinister self pity.

Rini stared at him with no discernible emotion, as his words were meaningless to her.

'I don't believe I know the lion tamer,' she said, after a moment's thought.

'I expect you will recognise him if I cut off his head and hang it at the gates for all to see?'

She took a second sip of wine, and boldly met the gaze of a man she had steered away from many uncharitable thoughts, although none as uncharitable as decapitation. Thus far.

'Why would you do that?' she said. 'I understood the greatest gift a king could bestow was his mercy.'

'Aha!' said King Arthur. 'You mean a *merciful* king is a *great* king!' He banged his fist on his empty banqueting table.

'I mean a merciful king is a great *man*,' said Rini. 'Or, at least, a good one.'

'A *good* man…' He waved his head from side to side as he took stock of her words. 'How many *good* men are equal to a *great* king?'

'One good man is worth ten great kings,' she replied. 'Because his goodness is grounded in humility and humanity, not the pomp and privilege of kingship.'

The wine had loosened her tongue to a pleasing effect. She returned her goblet to the table, and he refilled it with alacrity, his ruby ring glowing like the wine. Some distance away, a book fell from its lofty position on a shelf, followed swiftly by another, and finally, more deliberately, by a third. Their eyes locked together in mutual suspense, motes of dust, stirred by the commotion of the tumbled books, dancing between them in the shafts of light from the great domed ceiling.

She felt thrilled by her new-found sense of self in this strange new world where all she had known (including the knowledge that there was at least *one* other world out there!) was turning on its axis. But her abiding mission—that she must return to make things safe for Torran and Jade, and not leave them thinking they were abandoned to an uncertain fate—tugged at her insides.

They had both made for the fallen book, but her younger, smarter movements brought her more quickly to where it waited for them like another challenge. To her relief, he was amused by her victory.

'So, tell me, what will you be reading to me tonight, my love?'

The cold reality of her situation curdled within her, and her grip tightened around the book, before she chose to hide it in the folds of her dress.

'Your majesty, I crave your *patience*,' she said, and smiled sweetly, despite the pounding in her breast.

'My Rini!' he guffawed. 'You test me beyond reason, you perfect, imperfect little fool. I am told you still bleed despite the attentions of your king. I demand to know why you are still not with child?'

Her head spun with this new information about herself in Arthur's kingdom, her jaw ready to hang in disbelief, when their attention was turned to a knocking at the great door, and the arrival of company.

Clem, in front, strode towards them with such a lightness of bearing, her hands grasped dutifully together above her swishing skirts, that Rini's heart swelled again with joy at the sight of her resourceful old friend. Behind her, the man who had driven Rini's carriage to the castle, and another more burly character, were either side of a third man with his wrists tied, although he didn't give the appearance of someone who might be about to try and flee. His head was bowed, his hair hanging like curtains about to close on a face that was a picture of indifference despite the seeming seriousness of his situation.

Tam. The lion tamer! The extraordinary knowledge of this, and the fact he was the man she was deeply in love with, while being forced to entertain a needy, imperious old man, welled up in her and brought unwanted colour to her cheeks. He, however, didn't meet the glance that she hastily returned to the king.

'My humble servant,' the latter quipped, as Tam was released and shoved to the floor. 'I appreciate you bowing at my feet. It's the natural order of things, wouldn't you say?'

Rini was unsure whether this was directed at her, or the lion tamer, but neither was quick to respond.

'So, Rini,' the king continued, making a swaggering circle around Tam who remained on his knees, and prodding him with the toe of his boot. 'This is the very fellow of whom we were speaking. Is your memory refreshed?'

'Now I see who you mean,' Rini replied, determined not to falter. 'I believe we may have met.'

'Forgive me, your majesty,' Clem interjected, as Tam raised his head in readiness to speak. 'The clock is ticking, and it would be remiss of me not to remind you that this is an important night in Rini's moonscape. Her duty and mine is to make readiness for your coupling. You must feast, and she must be cleansed for you. Your majesty.' Clem bowed her head with practiced obedience.

Rini felt rooted to the spot, by the necessity of keeping her emotions in check as much as understanding her remit in this other life of hers.

'I am grateful for your good sense, wench,' said the king. 'Make haste, and we may even have time to watch this fool make sport with his cat before we make a *better* form of sport in the bed chamber.'

Once again, Clem fastened her arm around Rini's waist, in an attempt to move her swiftly out of the king's company, but not before they heard him add: 'I would like her better *lubricated* this time. I fear resistance is impeding our mission.'

*

'Fornication,' Rini said through gritted teeth, as her friend marched her back through the vaulted corridors to her room. 'He intends *fornication* tonight? Clem, I can't bear it…'

'Nonsense,' said Clem, who was already making ready Rini's toilette of potions and fresh underclothing. 'You have borne it with the fortitude of a woman worthy to bear the king's issue—at least until one *Tamwar* swept into town with the distraction of his circus act. I fail to see how bothering such a majestic animal and keeping it in captivity against the laws of nature could win anyone over, milady, never mind a person as remarkable as your superior self. Perhaps you could enlighten me?'

Tam and his lion were no match for the other thoughts that were teeming through Rini's brain at that moment.

'So it's true I have lain with that man before?'

Clem was going about her business too boldly to blush on Rini's account.

'My lady, I have marked every occasion in your notebook, as His Majesty requested. He may have taken His pleasure with most of the women at court, but He has been careful never to allow them to harvest His seed, until He decided on you, and it has become His abiding distraction. His heir will secure his place in the history of this land, His kingdom.' Clem paused, somewhat amused. 'Do you mean you've been somehow *oblivious* to his attentions?'

Rini remained as stock still while Clem disrobed her as she had been when she had dressed her earlier for her audience with the king. A bath had been prepared for her, perched on a mountain of glowing hot coals that a slight, cowering young woman was feeding with bellows while another poured jug after jug of water onto a sediment of herbs and flower petals.

'Clem, I have no remembrance of any of it. This life, here, is not where I belong. It's not who I truly am.'

'I thought that was just your addle-brain talking,' said Clem, who nevertheless shooed the other maids away for fear of gossip that might put one, or indeed all of them, in mortal danger.

'I must have been here, in some form, and I know your face, and that of the king, and Tam,' said Rini, a little desperately. 'But it's not where I'm present and *whole*. I'm sorry, it's the only way I can describe it.'

Clem seemed unmoved by her friend's speech, as Rini was now stripped naked before her, and she reached forward, awestruck, and placed her hands on her belly.

'Milady, look at you,' she said, softly.

Rini looked down at her body, seeing nothing remarkable, or so she thought, until Clem traced a finger from her navel to the top of the tightly curled hair at her groin.

'You have quickened,' said Clem, in amazement. 'You are with the king's child. Your blood spots must have been a baby taking root.'

'Root?' said Rini, in disbelief, but instinctively cupping her own hands round her gently swollen abdomen. 'And this, this is the *king's* issue? For certain?'

Clem laughed: 'Until your recent flit, we have had you under close guard, milady, so I don't think we can blame the carriage driver!'

'But I'm in love with someone else, Clem,' said Rini, as she was helped, shivering, into a bathrobe. 'I'm in love with Tam, the lion tamer. I know it, he knows it!'

'Milady, you haven't spoken two words to the lion tamer, nor him to you,' said Clem, with a surety that made Rini's heart sink. 'His majesty may be jealous of the idea of it, or of some stolen glances perhaps. But that is all that has passed between you. He is quite the enigma, with hardly a thought in his handsome head. Now, we must get you bathed and dressed. If you would like to give the king the good news He desires, you may be spared your night of *fornication*. Although,' she added, with a giggle, 'I've heard tell that He is quite the *satisfying* lover.'

'He's a bully and a fool,' said Rini, but too quietly for her friend to hear.

She was spared the attentions of the king that night. The news she was pregnant with his child was enough for him to grant her a night's rest while he drank deeply, and called for entertainment. The jollity of the servants in her earshot suggested to Rini that their king was very pleased with himself, and therefore with everyone else at court. Sleep eventually overwhelmed her, until she was woken rather roughly by Clem pulling at her bedclothes.

'Milady, the book! Where is the book?'

'What book?' said Rini, stirring heavy limbs and rubbing eyes that had been sealed in slumber. She remembered her audience with the king in his library, and joined Clem on her knees, rummaging though the litter of abandoned clothing at the foot of the bed. They found the book she had helped herself to earlier, she laying first claim, once again, until Clem forced it from her grip.

'He's livid,' said Clem, fighting to catch a breath. 'I must return it immediately, before He comes up here and…'

'Wait!' said Rini, sensing salvation. 'What's the book? Give it to me Clem, I beg you!'

Rini snatched it back, and thrust it under the lamp at her bedside to see what all the fuss was about. It seemed to be a map folded into book form, and a map that the king was clearly distressed to find in another's possession, even hers, his Favourite. *Especially* hers, perhaps!

'He's drunk, milady,' said Clem, hastily. 'But it won't take Him long to remember it was you who was with Him when it went missing today. He'll think you took it on purpose. He's ranting and raving!'

Rini understood in a blessed instant that the map was her way out of this kingdom, and back home to the world where she belonged. She was up and dressed in seconds, piling on layers and pulling on boots. She seized Clem by her wrists, and thrust her face up close to her friend's, so their fast-fighting breaths seemed to be competing with each other.

'Trust me, Clem! Do right by me, like I've always done right by you! By everyone I've ever known!'

Clem stared back, frightened, but seemingly willing, at last, to take Rini at her word.

'What must I do?' she said with a vulnerability that made Rini tremble inside for both of them, but she was undeterred.

'Help me get away from the castle. Bribe the carriage driver. Promise him anything! Tell Tam to turn the lion loose and cause chaos! We must get away quickly with this map until daylight can give us a clue where we're headed. Please, you're my only hope!'

*

As luck would have it, the erstwhile driver of the carriage was easily persuaded of his mission, as though being part of an adventure (anybody's adventure) was better than doing the miserable bidding, day after day, of a charmless, if not completely tyrannical, king.

Rini felt sad for the lion as their ears were filled with the shrieks of courtiers who heard tell it was on the loose in the castle, while the lion tamer was nowhere to be found. Clem told her she was in fact a lioness, although occasionally suffered the indignity of wearing a mane for theatrical effect, and was often seen curled up like a domesticated cat at the tamer's feet.

'I *do* believe I love him,' Rini said again to Clem, who simply shook her head, threw up her hands, and bundled her mistress back into the carriage that had borne her to—and now would speed her away from—King Arthur's castle.

When morning came and ushered in the favour of daylight, they spread the map out on their laps. It gave Clem no clue as to their mission, however Rini was able to trace their route back to the woods where she had taken her tumble, characterised by a black tree connected by a broken line to a wooden bench. She was as confident as she had ever been about anything that this was her way home.

'Wait for me, for ten minutes,' she told Clem, hugging her friend close as they alighted from the carriage. 'If I don't come back, then you can be sure you won't be seeing me again.'

Clem heaved a shuddering sigh as though she were fearful for both of them, for all of them, as the carriage driver sat leaning on his hands that held the reins, unsure of what might happen next, but utterly in thrall to these two errant women.

'Make him believe I escaped with the map, Clem,' said Rini. 'I've seen you; you can play him with the type of skill that I've seen you use to put out fires with one hand!' She reached for both of her friend's arms and twirled them wide, to Clem's confused amusement. 'Hide it somewhere safe and clever, should you ever have need of it. Tell him I said that his legacy should live on through *more* than his offspring. He should build more schools, open up his library, and give *everyone* the opportunity to go to the circus! *That* will make him a great king.'

They threw arms around each other, while the carriage driver's horse nodded noisily, rattling its harness once again in what might have passed for approval, but was more likely to be the creature's expression of boredom and dismay at the futility of human endeavours.

'What about the lion tamer?' said Clem, once she was let loose from Rini's embrace.

'Tell him I *will* see him again,' said Rini.

She took her leave of the team who had, in one brief pocket of time, been both her captors and her liberators; and picked her way through the

145

undergrowth to the blackened limbs of the tree that she believed would be there for eternity, and signified her passage home.

*

She wouldn't end up hating Art for this. She could never hate him on account of his fallibility and frailty, but it was with an overwhelming sense of gratitude and relief that she tumbled away from the world where he manifested himself as an overbearing monarch back to one where he was (in truth) now just a troublesome corpse.

TAM

She began looking at me with eyes of self-pity instead of her usual disdain, and I knew it was time.

I'd rehearsed this moment for what felt like a lifetime, but it still took my breath away, or, rather, made my breath come in uneven lumps, so that I had to sit down, blow and inhale, blow and inhale, until I didn't feel like I was going to faint with the enormity of it.

Mademoiselle. My missy, my puss-cat.

My she-demon, my tiger-lily, my terror.

In truth, the love of my life thus far.

It was time to make the kindest, hardest decision of this *my life thus far*, and I knew I needed the only other living soul I trusted to help me do it, to help me through it. Damn it, *to do it for me*.

I have no idea how many creatures will have sighed their last in the arms of Rini Sanchez, in the care of the only person on earth, I suspect, who could administer death and make it feel like a blessing. No doubt she would have kept her own tally, although I would hesitate to question her in case it sounded crass. I think I often sound crass. It comes from spending years with only a spiteful cat for company.

Watching her wrap the corpses of small animals for incineration has often given me pause: her hands moving deftly, and with a reverence that might have been afforded to the embalming of kings, her fingers tracing the labels on jars of foetuses suspended in fluid; tiny never-people whom she would nevertheless commit, one by one, to memory. She seemed cast as preserver and priestess in one.

I have wondered about my life as a Governor. I've moved uneasily among doctors and professors, preferring, if I'm honest, the company of the fellow in the market who sells me breakfast, or the woman in the subway who paints your portrait (not that she ever painted mine: I remained at her shoulder and merely marvelled at her skill, and our easy conversation)—or, of course, Rini the archivist.

Life has been mapped out for me, for all of us, and yet, for much of my life, I have felt like a charlatan, longing to break free from responsibility and good opinion to tread a humbler path, with a brush or a shovel in my hand, perhaps, instead of a pen and a test tube.

Rini has embodied her role with rare grace, never making me feel like I was taking advantage of her better nature. I strove not to be that person, but it hasn't always been straightforward, given my remit. It came a lot more easily to Dee while she was with us, playing her higher hand without compunction. She played me, too, of course, until, coming round with the sudden clarity of a rabbit no longer hypnotised by headlights escaping an untimely death, I took my leave of her, or, rather, stopped succumbing to the force of her passion for me.

Having gotten used to only serving dead animals in the form of tinned fish to Mademoiselle, I had never consumed so much fat and blood as when I was in thrall to Dee D'Abruzzo. It was an insane partnership, and I relinquished it without a backward glance. Fortunately, she recovered from this rebuttal with no discernible hard feelings, owing, I suspect, to my almost certain knowledge that her attachment to any man would only ever depend on the provision of his *attachment,* and the harder, the faster the provision he made, the better his fortunes would be. Particularly if he drew the requisite strength from the rare steak and calf's liver at her dinner table.

I think there comes a day of reckoning for a man like me who has cowered somewhat under the yoke of expectation. This day dawned when I gathered up my sickly princess, and took her to my place of work, via the basement entrance, for a clandestine meeting with my saviour Rini Sanchez.

I had classified her as someone who always played things by the book, although I've wondered if recent events had changed her. After all, the pandemic has changed all our lives at the laboratory, and elsewhere. It had even vanquished some. She made a note of all the drugs that she dispensed in a large brown ledger, printed out in her determined, left-sloping hand; and it would have felt anomalous and curiously weak of me to suggest an entry for drugs requested in my name for personal use, for my pet cat Mademoiselle, rather than, for example, Specimen XX000. But then again, why not? I was a Governor, and I could make any demand I wanted…

But Rini knew me better than that. We had shared more than cups of tea these past seasons, and our silences could have filled auditoriums with the mere suggestion of sound. She had loved and lost, and what should pass as my heart had broken for her, for her loyalty and commitment to a cause that she was prepared to accept was more worthy than any she might have conceived for herself. He was a Governor, of course, her lover Ben (Dee's brother-in-law, of all people), ready to take his advantage while he could. She became a surrogate mother to his child, and was then cast aside when his wife came home to reclaim her seat. She then did her time as a foster carer, deemed less deserving of a claim to parenthood than a houseful of other people who would surround the budding boy Torran with noise and know-how, but perhaps not the simple care and attention he craved—and she still gave She had helped find the lad a home with his grandfather (a grumpy old devil, as far as I could discern: probably a good match for Mademoiselle!), and was even on a mission to find the grave of the latter's old flame, so she could, as she explained to me, 'visit and lay flowers in his name'. A letter had arrived from the husband telling him she had died of 'a virus' that had laid waste to her weak lungs, but not before he had married her in her hospital bed. This seemed like bad luck, given all we have achieved; but Rini reminded me that it was a big world out there, and 'viruses were cleverer than people'. It seems she had taken more heed of Dee's preaching than I had given either of them credit for!

More than all of this, she was just Rini, my beloved friend, who took Mademoiselle to her breast, and spoke to her like she was a kitten about to embark on her first adventure chasing pigeons in the park, and who didn't flinch as tears washed down my face, and I was reduced to a trembling fool on my knees.

We wrapped her in a special blanket that Rini had brought for her—something I hadn't thought of, and yet this gracious gesture thrilled me like a final act of devotion for my girl, as her life ebbed away, witnessed with as much outward dignity as my inner state of devastation could muster.

We stood together in silent celebration of a life well-lived and relinquished surrounded by love; while Rini's newly rounding belly loomed between us like an undeclared but not forbidden truth. Our opportunity to talk about that would come. Whose lives, and loves, ever came without their complications, and were fractured in ways we couldn't begin to understand?

I took her beautiful brown hands in mine and kissed her, with simple longing, for the first time.

ARTHUR (IV)

The most peaceful time in the woods was when you were dead, he observed from the bench that had separated his worlds when he'd been alive.

Dead, or dying? It probably didn't make much difference, unless this was simply a holding bay while the decision was made whether he would go to heaven or to hell. If this was purgatory, he decided, then it wouldn't be such a bad place to stay in perpetuity.

Watching the world without the capacity to intervene may have troubled other mortals he had known, come this state of powerlessness, but for him, Arthur Smith, aged nothing no more, child of no one no longer, this was pure serenity.

He wouldn't call it Paradise, because he always imagined that would come with sunshine, and women in bikinis serving him an endless supply of potent drinks from coconut shells; but maybe it was, in fact, Heaven which, interestingly, wasn't the flip side of Hell.

There was a dog at his feet, and sometimes on his lap, of indeterminate breed (but probably a spaniel) that both administered warmth, and signalled the approach of strangers, by the frilling of its ears. Warmth, in death, was a curious feeling. It was like the aftermath of an orgasm, only it seeped into one's bones rather than out of one's body, leaving him with an unprecedented, indescribable sense of satisfaction.

Noley came by, he imagined in search of a headstone that she would never find, but she wasn't one for giving up easily if she were on a mission. Her fiancé Edward was in tow, trying to remain supportive. He couldn't help pausing, unseen (or so he thought!) to kick a tree out of frustration of loving a woman who would be forever inclined to be preoccupied with another man.

Arthur smiled at his good fortune at having been given an insight into what love and loyalty meant—the human, not the canine, kind—because he had been properly loved by Noley. She had done her time with him: she had toiled, she had tolerated. Surely that was what 'normal' love was all about?

He couldn't make Edward out clearly, either because Art had never seen him before, or perhaps because he didn't really want to. But the tree shook its black locks at him in response to his boot, losing none of its leaves in the process, and suddenly resembling more of a person than a feature of the forest.

It crossed his mind that this person-tree might be Amber, his youthful wife, with her wild mane of black hair, or their daughter Angelica recoiling in habitual anger—or his grandson Torran who had found himself too often at the boot end of life.

He made out the dark silhouette of Steve, his silent undertaker, brushing soil from the arms and legs of his clothing, and shaking out a tarpaulin that had no doubt been Art's makeshift shroud. He would have buried him, as instructed, in what appeared to be a no man's land comprising several yards of forest floor where Art had encountered neither man nor beast in his decades of exploring the space between his world and the next. Where better for his final resting place. Not for him a dreary graveyard where the dead were rounded up in regiments, much like they had been in life, but instead a private plot where he could decay in peace at the mercy of his own army of worms. Somewhere, he'd assured himself, that the circumstances of his demise would never be discovered, and with no one held to account for them.

He wondered if Steve would choose to return to the place that Rini had revealed to him was a passage to another world, the world where she had come from, along with the grandchildren who had now taken over his house! Knowing Steve, he would leave this knowledge in the past, along with his memories of the curious companionship they had shared for so many years, where actions largely assumed the job of words. He would have nothing to say, should questions ever be asked, about what became of Arthur Smith. He had sons of his own, and would no doubt leave the pushing of boundaries and the discovery of new frontiers to them.

At last came Rini, like a ship sailing serenely through the murky waters of his mortality. His heart (or where his heart used to be) felt drawn down to his bowels with misery at what he now knew to be her fate, for a while at least, at his hands. His latest world, this *after*-world, however, granted him no means to reach out to her to crave her absolution.

Presently, she was beside him, and her weight became his weight, his last breath shared with her as though they had become one.

This was her forgiveness for his temptation and trespass. All he could finally have hoped for.

Worlds without end.

Amen.

THE END

OTHER TITLES BY SASHA FAULKS

Trees and Men

The Wallet Pickers

The Last Thing at Night
First Thing in the Morning Pact

The Garrow Boy

Loving Amélie

Born Slowly

Soul Girl (children's fiction)

Short stories

A Dying Art

Ordinary Shorts

Printed in Great Britain
by Amazon

39796198R00096